LIVING WITH TEMPTATION NEXT DOOR
WILL HAVE HER BREAK ALL THE RULES.

FRIEND
ZONE

NICOLE
BLANCHARD

NEW YORK TIMES & USA TODAY
BESTSELLING AUTHOR

**PALM BEACH COUNTY
LIBRARY SYSTEM
3650 Summit Boulevard
West Palm Beach, FL 33406-4198**

Friend Zone

Copyright © 2018 by Nicole Blanchard

Bolero Books LLC
11956 Bernardo Plaza Dr. #510
San Diego, CA 92128
www.buybolerobooks.com

CONTENTS

To Atticus and Vyolette, sweet angels too precious for this earth, and their mother Mia, a great friend.

CHAPTER ONE

CHARLIE

THERE WAS no way to escape.

Trust me, I'd checked. The small half-bath had no secret doorways, and the window was so minuscule I couldn't fit through it even if I lost the pesky freshman fifteen I'd packed on two years ago. I opened it despite my misgivings and despaired at the slow progression. The air filtered in, clammy and thick, but my desperate lungs drew it in greedily. My fingers dug into the windowsill and I prayed for the first time in ten years. *Please, God, don't let me faint.*

The knock at the door made me screech, and I clapped a hand over my mouth.

"Charlie," came a familiar voice. "You okay in there?"

"Liam, how many times do I have to tell you not to interrupt me when I'm on a date?" I washed my hands and gave a quick look in the mirror. I frowned at my reflection. Limp

1

dirty blonde hair that fell rain-straight to my shoulders, plain brown eyes opened so wide I nearly scared myself.

Get it together, Charlie.

I opened the door and peered beneath Liam's raised arm. "Andrew didn't follow you, did he?"

"Why?" He sounded amused. I narrowed my eyes at him as I straightened. How could he be amused at a time like this? "What? I thought you got off on this part."

"What part? I don't get off on anything!" The screeching continued, and it was definitely coming from me. There must be something in the water. It wasn't like me to be so frantic and...unhinged.

Liam merely smiled that one-sided smile that made me want to sucker punch him. It made the dimple in his right cheek peek out to say hello. It was a tease, that dimple. It made most girls swoon, but it made me want to deck him because he only shared it with me when he was trying to piss me off, which he did with infuriating regularity. "Now, Charlie, you should know better than to keep breaking it off with these puppies if you aren't getting laid on the regular. Maybe that's why you're so uptight."

I looked to the ceiling. Maybe I'd find patience there. But there was no spiritual aid to be found, unless you counted the water stain that kind of looked like Jesus if I squinted just right. I'd grown sick of water stains. My dorm had them. My first apartment had them. What was it with college haunts and water-stained ceilings? One day I'd own my own home and there wouldn't be a water stain in sight.

"Focus."

I glared at him. "I am focused. Focused on not planting my fist in your face." I shoved around him, which wasn't easy considering how bulky he was. For a bartender-slash-veterinary student, he sure packed on the muscle. I guess it was hauling around all those kegs and delivering...I don't know calves or whatever it was he did at his family's farm that made him want to be a vet.

"Don't let your anger out on me because you aren't getting any." Liam followed close behind as I squeezed through the packed hallway of girls in skimpy dresses trying to get to the bathroom. Most of them side-eyed me until they caught onto the fact that Liam was much more interested in checking out their racks than paying any attention to me. After a lifetime of friendship, I was used to their reaction.

"I'm not angry."

"If I weren't getting laid, *I'd* be angry. Andrew must not be doing it right."

I spotted Andrew at the standing table where I left him, but paused instead of going to his side. I really hated this part. As I weighed my options, I said distractedly, "Then how do you explain the fact that you're a dick to me 24/7 if you're always getting laid? And Andrew is perfectly...nice."

"I'm not a dick," he said. My snort caused him to smile again, dimple twinkling. "Okay, well not all the time. Besides, I'm only like that with you because, you know, we're friends. The only time you should *really* worry is when I turn on the charm."

"You, charm? I doubt there's anything you could do that would ever make me forget what you were like at twelve with all your acne and that high-pitched voice. Sorry, buddy, there's no coming back from that."

Liam coughed and eyed a bombshell redhead who was giving him a sympathetic look. He leaned closer to me. "You promised me you'd never mention that again."

"And *you* promised you'd never interrupt another date."

"You can't be calling this a date," he replied, disbelief coloring his voice and expression. "Especially not if the sex is only *nice*."

My thoughts ground to a halt and I reached up to tug at my hair. "What do you mean by that?"

Redhead forgotten, Liam reclined against the wall next to me and jerked his head to where Andrew stood checking his watch. "You only bring a guy here when you've reached the dumping phase and I'm not about to give you a sex education lesson."

"Dumping phase? How did—what do—how did you know I was going to break up with him?" I stumbled through my response, my voice nearly giving out several times in my attempt to speak. "I don't need a sex lesson for you."

"Really? We've been friends for ten years. I think I know how this is going to go."

I rolled my eyes. "You have no idea how it's going to go." I paused, biting my lip. "Do you?"

Liam waved at his manager when he began to shoot him impatient looks. That was Liam, totally unconcerned about the fact that he was supposed to be actually *working*. It drove me almost as insane as his ability to see right through me did. "This isn't the first time you've brought a guy here when you want to break up with him and I doubt it'll be the last. What's the reason this time? You two have been kicking it for longer than usual. He do something stupid like propose?"

At my silence, he straightened and tried to keep a straight face. "Holy shit, did he propose?"

My hands knotted, and I looked away.

He snorted. "You're kidding." When I didn't answer, his expression grew serious. "Whoa. You're not kidding. Congratulations? I guess a lifetime of nice sex may be someone's idea of a happily ever after, though I'm not sure *who*."

For the first time in my life I understood the phrase about gazes shooting daggers and I wished mine would. He'd be dead ten times over. "Don't be ridiculous."

"Ouch. Poor guy. Now I actually feel bad for him."

I followed Liam to the bar and accepted the beer he offered. I figured I'd need more than one before the night was over and drank deeply, hoping the cool brew would soothe the dryness in my throat. "I didn't mean for it to go this far. We got along so well and he seemed to understand I wasn't looking for anything serious."

"This is what I mean about you and these guys. That's how I know you're about to break up with someone. You always bring them here. I almost feel bad for him," he said as he studied Andrew. "He has no idea you're about to break his heart."

"I don't break their hearts!" I sipped from my beer, contemplating his words. *At least, I don't think I do.*

Liam took an order from a couple who could barely keep their hands, and mouths, off each other while I worked up the nerve to walk over to Andrew and get it over with. It didn't escape my notice that I'd never been so into a man, Andrew or otherwise, who got me so hot I forgot we were in public. Maybe Liam was onto something about *nice* meaning something bad.

"Don't worry," Liam said when he was finished with the couple. "I'll keep an eye on him in case he freaks out."

"You're making this out to be a bigger deal than it is." Maybe if I repeated it enough, I'd start to believe it.

He leaned on the counter after handing me another beer. I hadn't even realized I'd downed my first. "C'mon, Charlie. You and I both know you've left a trail of men in your wake. It was only a matter of time before one of them got serious before you managed to shake them loose."

"You make me sound terrible." *Was I really that bad?*

"No, you're not that bad." He was smiling again at my habit of speaking my thoughts out loud, but this time at least I didn't want to punch him. This time I was thankful he was my best friend, so he could lie and tell me all the things I wanted to hear instead of the truth. "But you better let him down gentle."

I polished off my beer and accepted a third. I had a feeling I was going to need it. "Thanks for being here, Liam."

"Anytime, shortstack. Don't be too hard on yourself." He winked at me as he straightened. "Besides, you need someone who'll rock your world. Not someone whose *nice*."

"You're really asking for it," I told him.

I could only sigh as I made my way through the crowded bar to Andrew's side with guilt hanging like a heavy weight on my shoulders and settling uncomfortably in my stomach. It didn't help that when he heard me approach, Andrew turned to me with a wide, slightly wobbly smile on his face.

"There you are! I was about to come looking for you."

"I'm sorry I took so long. You know girls' bathrooms." I waved a hand, but he still mostly looks confused.

"I ordered you a cosmopolitan, but I see you've already gotten a drink." We'd been together long enough he'd memorized my drink order. It should have caused a pang of affection to chime in my chest, but there was...nothing. I frowned as he pushed the glass across the table. Noticing my expression, he asked, "Is something wrong?"

My smile wobbled and I downed half of the cosmo for liquid courage. It joined the beer already sloshing around in my stomach and the combination ignited. *Not a good idea,*

Charlie. I set the drink down and moved it out of reach. *Get it over with.*

"Actually, Andrew, there's something I think we should talk about."

He rolled his shoulders and shifted in his seat. "Good, I'm glad you mentioned it. There's something I wanted to talk to you about, too."

Caught off guard my throat closed on the words and I gestured for him to continue. A sense of foreboding settled over me like a dark cloud and I glanced around surreptitiously for Liam's comforting presence, but he was still busy at the bar. Besides, I didn't need him to come to my rescue. I could handle Andrew. *I hope.*

Andrew took my hand in his and all I could think about was how clammy it was. I had to resist pulling mine away. "You know how much I care about you," he said and tried to look deeply into my eyes. I hated when people did that. It always made me feel so incredibly uncomfortable. "We've been dating for a while now and..."

I couldn't take it anymore. I wasn't sure how I'd react if he actually proposed, but I knew it wouldn't be pretty. "Stop, Andrew. I think I know what you're going to say." My heart is beating triple time and I wouldn't be surprised if it leapt out of my chest and onto the table in between us—but not in a good way.

His shoulders relax and he sends me a grateful smile. "You do? Good. I was afraid we were on the wrong page."

Oh, you have no idea.

"I found the ring," I blurted.

His head jerked back so suddenly his whole chair moved with him, making an awful sound against the wood floors. People in our immediate vicinity turned in our direction. I wanted to melt into a puddle at the floor. I should have waited until we were in a private place. It hadn't even occurred to me he could make this into a scene.

"*What?*" I'd never heard his voice quite that high before.

I lowered mine in response, hoping to smooth his ruffled feathers before he got upset. "The ring. The engagement ring? I found it when I was at your apartment last week."

Silence filled the space between us and my ears began to ring, blotting out the sound of the bad karaoke from a couple of sorority girls in the corner. But over the ringing, I heard Liam's voice berating me for my love 'em and leave 'em attitude.

"You thought I was going to propose to you?"

Then it was my turn to gape at him like a fish. "Weren't you?"

His eyes flicked back and forth as he studied me. He leaned back and crossed his arms in front of his chest. "You were going to break up with me, weren't you?" He actually laughed and then leaned in across the table. "You were going to break up with me even though you thought I was going to propose."

The warmth from the alcohol curdled in my stomach. I

swallowed hard and pressed my hands into the table for balance. I wasn't going to throw up in public. I didn't even do that when I was fresh out of high school and acclimating to the constant flow of booze as a frosh. "You could do so much better than me, Andrew. I'm leaving this summer for a volunteer opportunity overseas. We wouldn't even get to spend a lot of time together." All my carefully rehearsed reasons now sounded pathetic and flimsy in light of Liam's accusations and the pure disbelief on Andrew's face.

He shook his head and got to his feet. "You're a real piece of work, Charlie. But for the record, I was never gonna propose to you. That ring is a family heirloom. My mom gave it to me last week for my twenty-fifth birthday."

I opened my mouth to respond, but he was already walking away. I downed the rest of the cosmo to wash out the bad taste in my mouth, but not even it could drown out the sound of Liam's words and Andrew's accusations.

CHAPTER TWO

LIAM

I KEPT an eye on their table as best I could, but the bar was packed on a Saturday night. By the time I looked up, I'd lost sight of them and their table was empty. As I filled drink requests for person after person my gaze flitted around the room trying find either of them. I cursed under my breath. Never should have let her do this on a night when I was working so I couldn't keep a close eye on her.

A half-hour later, it seemed half of the university had decided to show up so I hadn't been able to tear myself away. My eyes are gritty from the flashing lights and lack of sleep. I wish I could say it's because I've spent it with a woman, but I picked up extra shifts here and the pet rescue where I work as a vet tech for extra cash. If I was being honest it's been a hot minute since I've even had *time* for another woman.

The next girl in line, a pretty brunette with skin-tight

jeans and a killer smile, didn't even do anything for me. "Sex on the beach," she requested.

But it did nothing for me. Not even when she perched on the bar stool and arched her back to thrust her pretty breasts in the line of my gaze. "Coming right up," I told her. I was still focused on scanning the crowd to try and spot Charlie and her latest guy, so I only gave her breasts a cursory glance. The brunette pouted until I placed her drink in front of her and she flounced off for another target.

Normally, it didn't bother me that Charlie chose my job as her dumping ground. It kept her close in case something went wrong that way I could be there to handle things for her. But something about this particular one was making me twitchy.

"The hell's wrong with you?" asked the other bartender on duty. He was a pretty chill dude who played ball for Florida College named Tripp. I wasn't as into sports, but we got along well enough. He and Charlie lived in the same apartment complex and when I moved in next door to us, her friends along with Tripp always ended up hanging out together.

"What do you mean?" I leaned around the next customer to study a flash of blonde hair. *Not Charlie.*

"You're being twitchy."

I turned to him and grabbed the vodka for the drink I was making. "I'm not being twitchy."

"If you were any twitchier, I'd think you took one too many balls to the head."

The mental image produced by his words made me wince. "Charlie broke up with another one of her guys tonight. I've got a bad feeling about it, that's all."

Tripp snorted. "Are you sure that's the real reason?"

I started cleaning the counters between customers to keep my hands busy. *Twitchy, my ass.* "Of course it's the real reason. What else would it be?"

He elbowed me, knocking me off balance. He may be leaner than me, but it's all muscle, the little shit. "Can you think of another reason why you'd be so worried about who she's dating?"

"Aside from the fact that she's my best friend and I want to make sure she's okay?"

Tripp rolled his eyes as he prepped his next drink. "If that's what you want to tell yourself."

"That *is* the reason." I was pretty sure.

"I'm friends with Charlie and I've never been that concerned with her love life, let me tell you."

I wiped the counters again, even though they were still pristine. "I'm not concerned with her love life. Jesus, dude. I don't like the look of that Andrew guy and I've always kept an eye out for her."

"Sure, if that's what you wanna call it." He paused and gestured toward the counter. "Pretty sure it's clean enough."

"Fuck off," I told him as the next person stepped up to

order a drink. My body relaxed when I saw it was the man I was looking for. "Andrew. Hey, man."

His lip curled. "I need the key to Charlie's place. She said you'd have one. We broke up and I have some stuff of mine to get and she won't be going home for a couple hours. I want to get it tonight."

Relieved at the fact that he hadn't flipped his shit and having spotted Charlie by the end of the bar nursing another beer, I pulled the key off my ring. She'd let him borrow it before, so I didn't even think twice. I was more worried about checking on her. "I'm sorry to hear that. If you'll lock up and leave the key on her counter for her, that'd be great."

He left without another word after pocketing the key and wound his way through the crowd to get to Charlie.

"Why does she even go for those losers?" Tripp asked.

I shook my head. "She's determined to find the perfect guy for the perfect version of her life she has mapped out in her head. As soon as one of them shows a side that doesn't fit in with the man she's conjured up, she checks out."

"That's messed up. No one's perfect."

"Pretty sure she'd have the perfect guy and come up with an excuse to bolt," I said absently as I glanced back over at the two of them. Charlie's face was tense, her lips pressed together like she was holding back her words. Never a good sign.

"Still, maybe he was a good guy."

I took a step closer as I saw Charlie's face blanche of all

color. "If he were the right guy, he would have fought for her, you know?"

"Maybe he was scared."

"He had an engagement ring, she said. That normally means it's pretty serious."

I still didn't know how I felt about that. She dated and sometimes it got serious, but never permanent-serious. She'd never gotten close to getting engaged. I couldn't sort out why my stomach had dropped when she'd told me about the ring. Maybe it was the thought of things changing. Maybe it was the threat of losing my best friend. If Tripp had it his way, he'd say it's because I had feelings for her.

That couldn't be it.

Could it?

I shoved the thought away. There was no way in hell that had happened. We've been close for a long time, but it's always been platonic.

"You okay?" Tripp asked, no longer teasing.

I couldn't answer because I wasn't sure if I was. It was as though the Earth had shifted right under my feet. Everything around me was the same, but something intrinsic had changed. I just didn't understand what.

From the distance separating us, I could see a tear slip down Charlie's cheek and that broke me from my stupor. It didn't matter what was happening. She was clearly upset, and it was time to get her away from that guy, I didn't care if it pissed him off.

I didn't know what the hell he'd said, but it looked like she was about to full-out cry, which she never did...ever. Her face was red and her eyes bright with unshed emotion. The single tear she'd let go had left a shimmery trail down her cheek. He had her pinned in a corner against the bar and I could hear his outraged voice above the din, though I couldn't distinguish what he was saying from so far away. I found myself pushing through the crowd without another thought and was beside her in less than a minute.

"My mom was right about you," I heard him say as I got closer. "I never should have wasted my time on someone so worthless. I never would have proposed to you. I can't believe you'd even think so. Marrying you would have been the worst decision of my life."

"Ready to go home?" I asked Charlie. I paid no mind to the fuck-stain who turned to gape at me. As far as I was concerned, he no longer existed. I'd have Tripp cover the rest of my shift. If my manager gave me shit, I'd tell him to screw off.

Fuck-stain glared at me. "We're talking here."

Charlie's gaze skittered over to him, but I cupped her chin and brought it back to me. "Let's go home," I said, my tone gentle. "I'll pick you up some wine and we'll watch all the chick shit you want." A huge concession, considering I loathed all those girlie movies. My mom and sisters watched them non-stop growing up and sitting through one was enough to make me hurl.

Fuck-stain scoffed and glared some more, and I wondered how I'd ever thought he was good enough for her. Until further notice, *no one* was good enough for her. He was lucky I didn't put my fist in his face.

"I'd rather watch an action movie," she said. The corner of her mouth tilted up, and if it hadn't wavered, if there hadn't been the slightest glimmer of sadness in her eyes, I wouldn't have done what I did next. We would have gone out, grabbed some wine and food, and continued with our lives the way they were.

But it was that show of vulnerability that hit me right in the gut. She was hurting and all I wanted to do was take her up in my arms and make it go away. This guy had beat her down, torn up her self-esteem, and when she'd stood up to him, he hadn't been able to handle it.

"I'm ready to go," she said and squared her shoulders, but I was still staring at her mouth.

Fuck-stain made an angry noise in the back of his throat, but neither of us were paying any attention to him.

Ignoring him, my own objections, and common sense, I closed the distance between us and pressed my mouth to hers.

After a moment of surprise where her body froze against mine, her lips parted with a little moan, and it burrowed deep down inside me and took root. All I could think about as we were pressed together was how right it felt. She leaned against me, her breasts pressing against my chest, and I slid a hand down to the small of her back to keep her close. My senses both sharpened and dulled at the same time. Everything involving her was crystal clear, but everything else—the pulse of the music, the dull roar of conversation, even her fuckin' ex—all faded to the background.

There was only her. It had taken me most of my life to really see her. And now it was like I only had eyes for her.

CHAPTER THREE

CHARLIE

LIAM WAS KISSING ME.

Liam. My best friend.

What the fuck?

"What the fuck?" Andrew echoed.

I pushed Liam away after a long moment and turned my head, unable to process what had happened. His harsh breathing sounded like he'd run a marathon, whereas I seemed to forget how to breathe altogether. The alcohol made my head spin and the repeated sound of Andrew shouting was giving me a headache.

"Can you not?" Liam said. His body vibrated against mine. I chanced a look and would have pulled back if it weren't for the hand he had pressed against my back. I'd never seen him so furious.

As my body relaxed, he pulled me even closer. He was protecting me, like he had since the day my mother abandoned me with my dying father. My assumption was confirmed when he let go of me to push me behind his back. From the view over his shoulder, I could see Andrew fuming, his face red and his hands fisted at his side.

"Screw you." Andrew's voice shook and a vein pulsed at his temple.

"Just go, man," Liam snapped. "We're done here."

Andrew's eyes turned cold, determined. "Not even close."

Liam kept me tucked behind him until Andrew pushed his way through the crowd, then he turned and cupped my face with both hands. "God, I'm sorry. You okay?"

"Well, I guess you were right," I mumbled.

His thumbs traced my cheeks in one last lingering touch and then he pulled me away from the curious crowd to a pair of empty bar stools. He tugged me onto one and braced an arm on the bar. We were sitting so close I could hear him above the music and shouted conversations. It reminded me of how it felt when his body was pressed against mine and I shivered.

"About what?" he asked. His lips glistened in the glow of strobe lights. I'd never paid attention to them before, but now I knew what they felt like. I couldn't help but wonder, despite everything, what it'd be like to feel them on mine again.

I shook my head at the memory of his heat wrapped around me. The kiss was a way to get Andrew to back off.

That's all. "That I break their hearts. I never would have done this here if I'd known he would cause such a scene."

He scowled. "Don't apologize for that dipshit. He's only upset because he knows what he's missing."

I sniffled and wiped at my eyes. *I was* not *going to cry*. "He wasn't going to propose. Didn't you hear? I'm not good enough for his perfect family. I don't know why I keep dating. It's a good thing I'm leaving after this semester."

Liam straightened. "You're what?"

All I wanted was to go home—not the little apartment I rented near school—but home, where Liam and I grew up. It's funny, my mom had run out on us when dad got sick when I was thirteen and I'd always promised myself I'd never turn out like her. I guess some things run in the family.

"I was going to tell you later, but I got offered an opportunity to volunteer overseas. They need nurses to give vaccines, run free clinics. That sort of thing."

He rocked back on his stool and rubbed a hand over his face. "Wow, Charlie, that's great."

"Thanks. I'm sorry I dragged you into all this. Next time, I'll make sure to find another place to break up."

His gaze met mine. "Next time?" Was it a trick of the dim lighting or was he upset?

The heat in his eyes prompted the memory of the kiss. I had to knock it out of my brain before all I could do when I was around him was think about kissing him. "Well, probably not since there's no point in dating if I'm leaving soon anyway." At his silence, I kept babbling. "Anyway, thank you for jumping in. Kissing me was probably a better choice than punching him and getting fired. He was so sure you and I had something going behind his back, so it must have pissed him off something bad. Joke's on him though, right?" I attempted a smile, but I could only muster up a grimace. This was why friends never kissed. It made everything awkward as hell. I could only hope our friendship would survive it.

He looked away and eased himself back. "A joke. Right."

Silence filled the space between us and I didn't like it. There had never been space in our friendship before and I hated to be the reason there was now.

"Liam, is everything going to be okay?" My voice trembled, but I carried on. "I don't care about Andrew, but I can't lose you. I know you were trying to protect me. You're a good friend. Can we just...go back to the way things were?" Somehow I'd gotten my hands on a cocktail napkin. I looked down in my lap to avoid his expression as he considered my words. The napkin was shredded in a pile on my thighs.

His hand covered mine as I began to shred the pieces into even smaller ones. I looked up and found him smiling at me, the traces of awkwardness gone. "It's alright. I was protecting you, like you said. Besides, I'd never let a douchebag like him mess with us. We're good."

I slumped and laughed, but it was shaky. For a second there, I thought maybe he'd been seriously hurt. For a second there, I'd even given half a thought to what it'd be like to kiss him on a regular basis. Then, I remembered what he said about me breaking hearts. I'd never want to hurt Liam. He was the most important person in my life. "Good. You had me worried."

"Naw, it was only a kiss."

"It wasn't even a good one," I said with a smile to soften the burn as I gathered the remains of the mutilated napkin and left it on the counter. Joking seemed easier than acknowledging the I hadn't wanted the kiss to end.

Liam grinned back at me and I knew everything between us would be okay. At least until I left, but I'd worry about that later. "Now I know you're talking out of your ass," he said. "Do you want to get out of here?"

I pressed a hand to my aching head and nodded. "What about your shift?"

"Screw it. I'll have Tripp cover for me. He owes me for when I switched with him for his tournaments."

"Are you sure?" Part of me needed space, but another more dominant part wanted me to cling to Liam for all I was worth. Tonight had shaken me down to my core and the thought of going home alone scared me more than it should. I knew it wasn't the same, but I couldn't help but remember the night I came home after a volleyball game and the house had been empty, my mother nowhere to be found.

He gave me a look that said don't be stupid and said, "I'll get my stuff if you want to meet by my truck."

I nodded and my stomach nearly dropped to my feet as

he got to his and paused to kiss my forehead before disappearing into the mass of throbbing bodies. I almost thought he was going to kiss me again.

Cut it out, Charlie.

If I wasn't already sick from the four drinks I already had, I would have ordered another to steady my nerves. I'd never been so off-balance around Liam before. It had been a long day, that was all.

I slung my purse over my shoulders and navigated through the crowd to the door. The slap of fresh air against my face helped to clear my head. Clusters of giggling girls clung to each other as they navigated their way up the busy streets. A niggling worry at the back of my head had me pulling out my phone and unlocking it just in case. I didn't think Andrew would be waiting for me, but I'd rather be cautious. I never thought he'd explode the way he had, either. I let go of the breath I was holding when I got to Liam's truck in the well-lit parking lot by the back door.

There were a few tense moments where I was certain I'd see Andrew emerge from the shadowed streets beyond the parking lot, but I brushed them off. Liam pushed through the back door to the bar, followed by a short burst of music and laughter. The door slammed and his boots crunched in the gravel to the truck.

"Are you sure you won't get any trouble for leaving early?" I called out.

"Jesus, fuck, Charlie, who are you my mother? I said it's fine. Now do you want a ride or not?"

Remembering the creepy suspicion Andrew was watching, I nodded. "Yes, of course. Thanks."

You know what?" he asked as he unlocked the truck and we jumped in.

I was already feeling better as the familiar surroundings of his old truck soothed my nerves. "What?"

"Maybe we should go home for a couple of days," he suggested, revving the engine. "That way you can take your mind off things for a bit. I'm sure my family would love to see you."

I rolled my eyes and frowned at my lap. I wanted to go more than anything, but I didn't want to seem needy either. "I have class next week. I'm not sure that's a good idea."

"Well, you don't have a say in the matter," he told her and pulled out onto the street. "You've got shit in our spare room. I'll call my mom and let her know we're on our way."

"You don't have to do this, you know," I said.

He palmed my head with one hand and shoved. "Don't be stupid."

"Yes, sir," I said, and relaxed. This was the Liam I was used to. Maybe I'd imagined everything else.

It gave me hope that it wouldn't be as hard to go back to normal as I thought it would be.

∾

"DON'T DO IT," I begged an hour later.

Liam grinned and quirked his eyebrows, his dimple making an appearance. I was back to wanting to slug him. "Are you sure?"

"I'm begging you, please, Liam. No."

"Just one more."

I righted myself in the seat and turned in his direction. My eyes narrowed in warning. "If you skip through another song without listening to it all the way through, I will personally rip the radio out and throw it in the nearest swamp as gator bait."

He gasped, and his hand dropped from the controls. He looked as offended as he had when I forced him to wear a pink tie to prom to match my dress. "You wouldn't dare."

"Try me," I said through gritted teeth.

His lips pulled into a smile and we both jumped when the car behind us laid on the horn. He snorted out a laugh and hit the gas. "You win for now."

"Seriously, I don't understand how you listen to music that way. You never finish a song. What's the point? And don't you dare quote *Supernatural*! You're the one who dragged me on this trip, so shotgun gets to pick the music."

"Fine, fine. This one time you can choose."

He patted my knee and I flushed at the feeling of his palm on me. It may have been through the fabric of my jeans, but now that my body knew how he felt in other places it was like I couldn't stop thinking about having his hands on me...

everywhere. I swallowed, hoping my voice wouldn't betray my thoughts. "You're such a good friend," I said, more to remind myself than him.

"Don't make me regret this," he warned. The twangy plucking of guitar strings filled the truck ear, and he sighed heavily, removing his hand. "Charlie."

I frowned at the disappointment that flooded me. Maybe going with him so soon after hadn't been such a good idea. Even though I was afraid of losing him this summer, the last thing I needed was to be cooped up in a small space with him and wishing he would touch me. I tried to refocus on the banter that had always come so easy to us, but any conversation took monumental effort. "Don't judge, Walsh. You focus on the road and let the DJ handle the tunes."

"I'm already regretting it," he said. Thankfully, he didn't seem to notice my inner turmoil. I should be thankful, but in the back of my mind I wondered how he could be acting so normal after what had happened.

I flicked a glance in his direction and cast out a mental net for another safe topic of conversation. One that didn't involve tongues, or hands, or close spaces. "Was your mom okay with us coming over?" I asked. There. His mom was *definitely* a safe topic. She loved me, but I'm certain she wouldn't think too kindly if she knew the thoughts I was having about her son.

"Yes. She said she's looking forward to seeing the both of us. She wanted me to remind you that you promised to help her weed the garden and she's holding you to it while you're visiting."

I went quiet for a few minutes as I scrolled through his phone and tried to think of something else to say. His playlists numbered in the thousands and it always made me smile to tease him about how he hoarded music like I hoarded chocolate. I glanced up to study him as he drove. The glow from the dash illuminated the strong, clean lines of his face. His close-cropped hair was now covered in a baseball cap, Braves I bet. He was a die-hard fan. My heart squeezed inside my chest and I looked back down at his phone.

He flicked my ear and I scowled up at him. "You hear me?" he asked.

I rolled my eyes. "Yes. God, Liam. I heard you."

"You don't have to call me God," he said with a smirk.

Despite my worries, laughter bubbled up from my throat. "You're so full of yourself."

He tugged on one lock of hair framing my face. "That's why you love me."

My response stuck in my throat and I could only smile shakily.

I loved Liam, I did. But I didn't *love* him.

Right?

CHAPTER FOUR

CHARLIE

SOMETHING TICKLED my face and I groaned, trying to bat it away with one hand.

"Charlie."

"Ugh," I mumbled, and turned my face away from the annoyance.

"C'mon. Char. We're here."

I cracked open one eye and tried to invest as much of my burning hatred into my glare as possible. "Here, where?"

"My parents' house," Liam said in an over-exaggerated voice. "Just a quick warning. Grandma Dorothy isn't doing so well, so she moved in with them a couple months ago."

That cleared the cobwebs from my brain. I sat up straight, nearly knocking heads with Liam, who dodged back just in time to avoid the collision. The fear for his grandma, who was as much my own, erased most of the earlier awkwardness from earlier. At least for now. "What do you mean, she's not doing so well? Why didn't you tell me?".

A shadow of emotion crossed his face, but it was gone too quickly for me to decipher. "Her dementia got worse. The doctors recommended she either go to a nursing home or we get her full-time care. Mom didn't want to put her in a nursing home yet, so they hired a service to help take care of her here."

I pushed a hand through the flyaway hair that had come loose sometime during my nap. Grandma Dorothy had been as much a part of my adolescence as Liam's, considering how much time we spent together after my mother left and my father got sick. My aunt's house wasn't exactly a refuge, even though she raised me after my dad died, so I treated Liam's place as a sanctuary. Thankfully, his family took pity on my gangly self and fed me regularly. They even came to graduation with one of those cheesy poster board signs with my name on it.

"Did your parents not want you to tell me?" I asked, my voice so low I wasn't sure if he could hear me or not.

He did a double take. "What? No. It wasn't like that at all." He paused before continuing. "She called before everything with fuck-stain and I didn't get the chance to tell you."

"Fuck-stain?" I didn't want to touch that one, so I said. "What did your dad say?"

Liam scowled. "The same thing he always says. That I should come back to work for the family. That going to school is only going to put me into debt. The family could use me at home to help with chores and take care of her. The usual."

"I wish you would have told me. I wouldn't have said yes to coming if I knew things were still bad between you two."

He gave me the same look he used to when I was being particularly boneheaded. "Don't you dare say that. I didn't just do it for you. If grandma is as bad as Mom said then I want to be here to spend time with her and I knew you would, too. So get your ass out of the car before I drag you out."

I wanted to protest. I even opened my mouth to start, but the more I thought about it, the more I realized Liam was right. Without looking up, I said, "I didn't mean to--"

Liam nudged my chin up with his hand. "You don't have to apologize, Char. Trust me. I wasn't kidding about dragging you out. I may even throw you over my shoulder if I have too, which may give grandma a heart attack," he added with his customary wicked grin.

I smacked him on the arm, grateful for the broken tension. If he was going to ignore the kiss, then I was, too. It's the only way things will go back to the way they used to be. "Let's get inside before I have to murder you on your front lawn and your mom has to clean up the mess."

"Remember that time we TP'd the street and she made us take it all down?"

We shared a laugh as we started walking up to the front

door. "I thought we were never going to get that shit out of the branches. We were up there for hours."

"It was your idea to do my house," he argued. "I knew it was gonna come back and bite us in the ass."

"You liar! You're the one who said they'd never suspect us!"

By the time we reached the front steps we were both giggling, and I smiled for the first time since the night before. The heaviness was still present, waiting for the moment when I let my guard down and it could take over, but for now, I had Liam to distract me and if he was good at anything, it was distraction.

"Suspect you for what?" came a voice that sucked the laughter right from our lungs.

"How much I missed you," I said as I opened the creaky screen door to get a better look at her. I had to force the words passed the lump in my throat. "Hi, Mrs. Dorothy. It's so good to see you."

Grandma Dorothy stood behind the screen door. I wish I could say she looked the same, but the ravages of time were more evident than ever. I swore she was a good three inches shorter, her spine curved and requiring her to stoop over. The thin curls she religiously colored a soft brown every eight weeks had thinned and lost their bounce. My heart squeezed. How had I let so much time pass since the last time I visited? I knew the answer, I just didn't want to admit it to myself. I'd gotten so used to leaving people before they could leave me, I was doing the same thing with Grandma Dorothy that I'd done to Andrew. And neither of them deserved it.

After a quick look at Liam for reassurance, I wrapped my arms around her frail body for a hug. The familiar scent of peony body spray filled my nose and instantly caused the tension inside me to loosen. *Home*, it said. Finally.

I hadn't realized how much I'd missed it until Dorothy said, "Well, get inside. You're letting all the cool air out."

I giggled and released her to let Liam inside. He stooped down to give her a kiss on her papery cheek. He was so much taller than her that she had to lean her head way back to see him. The sight of them together pulled at me in a softer, sweeter way than kissing him had. My breath caught in my throat and Liam glanced at me, his eyebrows drawing together. I shook my head.

Grandma Dorothy interrupted the moment and I was thankful until I heard her words. "Willy, is that you? My, you've grown two feet if you've grown an inch."

The two of us froze and stared at each other with wide eyes. Liam was named after his father. William Walsh, Sr., who everyone called Willy. They'd shortened William to Liam to differentiate the two.

I watched as Liam's throat bobbed and his eyes softened as he stooped down to her level. "No, Grandma. It's me, Liam."

Dorothy shook her head and beckoned us to follow down

the hall. "I know that, silly goose. Let's go find your mother so we can tell her my two favorite people are home."

I took Liam's hand despite the fact that I couldn't stop thinking about the kiss when I touched him. No matter what weirdness was going on between us, sometimes he needed me to protect him, too.

CHAPTER FIVE

LIAM

WITH HER HAND IN MINE, I could face seeing my father.

Grandma Dorothy went to the fridge and began pouring tea. When I noticed her hands shaking too much to hold the pitcher steady, I went to her side.

"I'll get that for you grandma." I took the pitcher from her hands and guided her to the breakfast nook where she sat across from Dad. He hadn't looked up from the paper he was reading. A steaming cup of coffee sat as his elbow.

She beamed up at me. "You're a good boy. Thank you, Willy."

"Anytime." I told her, deciding not to comment on her error about my name. Ignoring the issue wasn't healthy by any means, but it was better than focusing on how quickly she had changed. To Charlie, I said, "Do you want a cup?"

Charlie gave my hand an extra squeeze, then took an empty seat next to Grandma Dorothy. "Sure, thanks."

"Hey, Dad," I said when I couldn't put it off any longer.

"Liam," was all he answered. *Was it just me, or did he look...older?* I didn't want to believe it. In some ways, I still wanted to think my father was invincible.

I poured iced tea for the three of us and served them. "How have you been, grandma?" I asked to break the silence. Sometimes silence was worse than my father's dictating to me. His blatant lack of interest in having a conversation screamed how little my life mattered to him these days. But, oh, how he'd come to life if only I did everything right—which meant his way or nothing at all.

"Just fine, dear. How's school?" Under the table, her foot began to tap against the floor and when her hands weren't busy with the glass they were constantly rubbing together. Once we'd learned she'd been diagnosed with dementia, the first thing Charlie had done was look up all she could about dementia. She quizzed her nursing instructors, scoured any available medical texts and gracefully agreed to help advise my parents when they chose home health care, even though she didn't think she was experienced enough to be of any assistance.

I always thought I was the one who took care of Charlie, protected her...but she did her fair share of taking care of me, too.

"Just waiting to hear back about applications for school in the fall."

My father snorted into his coffee and set down his newspaper. The full force of his gaze turned to me, pinning me to the sink where I was rinsing the empty pitcher. I'd been right earlier, he does look older. But that wasn't the only thing. He looked like an older me. Was this what I'd turn into if I spent the next thirty years fighting to pull life from an unforgiving patch of earth? His weathered skin had deep grooves that reminded me of cracked mud when the farm went too long without a good rain.

I ignored him because I didn't want another argument in front of Charlie and grandma. Raised voices agitated her.

"That's great," Grandma said, beaming. "What about you, Charlie?"

Charlie smiled at her, her cheeks pink with pleasure and she told grandma about her classes and the kids she saw on rotation at the hospital during her rounds. I'd forgotten how much she loved behind here. She even said once being around my family, even when they fought, was like a relief for her. I relaxed a little, ignoring Dad's scrutiny. I could deal with his bullshit for one weekend if it gave Charlie a reprieve.

"Where are Janie and Marie, Mr. Frank?" Charlie asked my dad. She never had a problem talking with him and he treated her like a third daughter.

"They're sleeping over at a friend's house for the weekend."

"I was wondering why it was so quiet," she said, eyes twinkling.

He mustered up what passed for a smile in her direction

and it hit me how Charlie always manages to pull people out of their shell, even miserly old bastards like my dad.

"Those two do more caterwauling than the barn cats."

Grandma was tapping her feet again and Charlie reached over to hand her the glass of tea without a second glance. My father looked at Charlie with such warmth in his eyes and Grandma Dorothy began chattering happily about the t.v. programs she'd been watching, I leaned against the kitchen counter, my heart stuck in my throat. Charlie fit. I couldn't imagine being here without her.

I wanted to kiss her again.

The urge slammed into me with the intensity of an avalanche. I wanted to cross the kitchen, pull her to her feet and plant a kiss on her she'd never forget. Not a hasty, spur-of-the-moment kiss. Right here in front of my family, alone. It didn't matter where. I wanted her. And it terrified me.

"Did you hear me son?"

I focused in on my father, who was standing in front of me, his coffee cup in his hand. That was one way to get my thoughts off the carnal route they'd taken. "What's that?"

"I could use your help outside, if you have a minute."

It shamed me, as it always did, that my first response was to tell him no. I didn't want to spend the whole weekend doing chores and listening to him gripe about how I was abandoning the family to get a degree I didn't need. Then I took another look at those new lines on his face and relented. Besides, it'd get my mind off kissing Charlie, or at least, I hoped so. She has enough on her plate with what went down with Andrew and now she was leaving in a couple months. *Forget about it, Walsh.* I'd be content with the way things were. I had to be.

"Sure, dad. I'll be outside in just a sec."

He nodded, reached around me to put his cup in the sink, then pushed out the squeaky back door, the screen slapping behind him.

I crossed the scuffed checkerboard linoleum to the table and stopped to give Grandma Dorothy a kiss on her hair. I met Charlie's eyes over grandma's head and said, "Will you be okay here for a little while?"

She smiled, but there were questions in her eyes. "Sure. I bet Grandma Dorothy and I can find something to keep us plenty busy."

"You sure?"

Grandma twisted in her seat. "You heard the girl. Now get outside. Your daddy's been busting his back for months, but he's not as old as he used to be and could use your help."

Charlie sent me a sympathetic look and I sighed. Sometimes, despite her patchy memories and tics, Grandma could send an arrow straight through to the bullseye. "*Go,*" Charlie mouthed.

It wasn't that I didn't want to help my family. I wanted to, I tried. But living my father's life wasn't *all* I wanted for my own. I had my own dreams. My own goals. He was stubborn enough that he didn't want to bend, and I was stubborn enough that I'd never ask for help.

I found him in the old barn situated a healthy walk behind the house. Whatever color it had been painted when it was new had long since faded. My dad, and sometimes I, had kept it in good repair as best we could. Replacing the roof, rotted beams, weathered siding. It was a patchwork mess but the scent of fresh hay for the horse and motor oil was a familiar and welcome reminder of all the years I'd spent here. I thought of Charlie, who'd come to love my family in place of her own and felt guilty about even wanting to run from this place.

Dad called out from where he was sprawled underneath a tractor. "You're taking your sweet time, aren't you?"

Still thinking of Charlie, I swallowed my angry reply and hunkered down with one hand keeping balance on the side of the rusted old machine. "What do you need?"

We were more alike than I wanted to admit, because I saw him choke on his own response before he bit out, "Get me that wrench there."

Like they'd been a thousand times before, the tools he needed for the job were laid out on a towel, a dirty one, but as organized as you could get in a country barn. I found the wrench and passed it to his outstretched hand. Metallic clanks echoed throughout the bowels of the tractor.

It would have been so easy to be the son he wanted me to be. Easy in that I could see how much he wanted the kind of man who'd proudly carry on the traditions he'd started, who'd farm the land he slaved over his whole life. The irony was it was the very farm that had inspired me to become a vet. We had horses, donkeys, a cow or two, plus a slew of chickens, goats and barn cats. It wasn't out of the ordinary to have the large animal vet visit a couple times a year. Dad hadn't thought anything of my tagging along back then, but it had molded me in the way that I knew he still wished the farm would.

The conversation we should have been having hung over the rest of the afternoon like a dark cloud, but neither of us could make the first move. Instead, the only words spoken were requests for more tools or polite small talk. I wished as I handed him a screwdriver and followed his directions for guiding in a part that I could talk to him like I had when I was a kid. Then he'd ask for something else and the moment was lost.

It wasn't until he slid out from under the tractor that he looked me in the eye for the first time since I got home. He wiped his hands with a rag and sighed. My body tensed in preparation.

"We're selling the farm," he said.

CHAPTER SIX

CHARLIE

"I'M SO happy to see you again," Mrs. Walsh said as she smiled at me over a glass of milk after dinner that night. Liam had come in after a couple hours with his dad looking like a thunderstorm rolling in, so I kept my distance. He'd only surfaced when his mom started making dinner with a healthy side of homemade chocolate cookies. "I kept telling Liam he needed to bring you around."

A pang of guilt made my stomach clamp down on the contents of rich chocolate-y goodness. "I know. I'm sorry I haven't visited. I've had...a lot going on."

She tutted at me. "No need to apologize, honey. Liam told me all about the boy you've been seeing. Andrew, right? How's that going?"

Liam, who'd been happily stuffing his face with his mother's homemade chocolate chip cookies, paused, and his eyes came to me. I shook my head subtly, and he chugged a glass of milk to help the cookies down.

I shrugged in his mother's direction. "It's going alright." I hoped my response was nonchalant enough. Mrs. Walsh had a bullshit detector like you wouldn't believe.

Which was why when she said, "Now, I don't believe that for a second, but I'll let it slide until you're ready to talk about it, sugar bean," I couldn't look her in the eye. "Don't you worry," she added, "these things have a way of working themselves out."

"I sure hope so," I managed.

"You two clean up after yourselves. I'm gonna check in on Grandma Dorothy."

"Thank you, Mrs. Walsh," I said.

"No need, honey. You're family."

She stopped to kiss us both on the head like we were twelve instead of twenty-two, and I realized I needed this much more than I thought I would. I turned to Liam, who was licking the chocolate off his fingers. I ignored the pang of heat the sight ignited in my stomach and focused on my own cookie.

"Thank you for this," I said around a mouthful. "How did you know it was what I needed?"

He shrugged. "I didn't. I just tried to think of the one place that makes me feel better when something bad happens, and this was what came to mind. Besides, I had a wicked craving for homemade cookies, and I figured you wouldn't be open to baking for me."

We both knew he was joking, but I was grateful for the change of subject. "You're such an asshole."

He batted his eyes. "But you love me."

"Debatable," I said, but I was smiling. He had a knack for making me smile when I absolutely did not want to. We'd be in the middle of arguing about God only knew what and he'd start cracking joke after joke, because—as much as he wanted to win the argument—he wanted me to smile more. Or so he said. "What are we doing today?"

"Since chores are done and dad can't guilt me into helping out anymore on Mom's orders, I have a surprise," he said, then rounded the table to pull me from the chair and push me out the back door to the attached garage. "No time for thinking right now. If you start thinking you'll overthink it, and I can't handle the drama."

At first, I thought he was talking about the kiss and then I realized he must be talking about Andrew. I really needed to stop thinking about ways to go in for round two.

"Are you going to tell me what you and your dad talked about this afternoon?" I blurted out. *Great job, Char. Real subtle.* "You came back looking like he was drowning kittens or something."

"Long story. We can talk about it when we get where we're going."

I stumbled in the darkened garage, my hands outstretched

to keep from running straight into something. "Where in the world are you taking me? Liammm. I do *not* want to go skinny dipping again."

He snorted and then placed his hands on my shoulders to guide me. I heard the rattled groan of an old truck door opening followed by a waft of leather, grease, and earth. "Scoot in," Liam said, and gave me a little heave into the cab of the truck.

"Umph," I grunted. It was his father's old truck. The one they used during the summer to tend to his part-time handy-man business in addition to all the work they did on the farm. "Is this going to be a theme? You shoving me into vehicles and taking me off on a whim?"

"It would be if you'd shut your trap."

"I can't help it. I'm not the ride-or-die type. I have too many questions."

"Clearly," he replied as he hit the button for the garage door opener, then backed the truck into the driveway.

Before I could ask any more questions, he'd thrown the truck into Drive and we were bouncing along a rutted country backroad. The sound of night birds filled the truck over the smooth crooning from the latest country star. Being down one sense heightened all the rest and despite my constant reminding, my brain was especially attuned to how close Liam and I were on the bench seat.

"Should I be worried?" I asked to cover my nerves. This was *Liam*. I've known him forever. I shouldn't be nervous. It was like we'd crossed a line into a different territory and my eyes were open to things I'd noticed, but not at this level, not with this amount of intensity.

"You know I'd never let anything happen to you," he said.

"I know, but you've also never done anything like this before."

"I had a feeling we could both use a break."

The truck eased to a stop with a squeal of breaks. We unbuckled, and Liam tugged me into his arms and carried me to the back of the truck where he tossed me bodily into the bed. A godawful, scream-queen-worthy screech ripped from my throat as I sailed through the air and landed, not on the hard metal like I was expecting, but on soft, downy fabric.

"Listen, Walsh," I said when I finally caught my breath, "I appreciate you kidnapping me and throwing me around, but I have to say, your attempts to cheer me up leave a lot to be desired."

The truck creaked as he heaved himself over the side and plopped down next to me. "Shut up for a minute and just look."

"Look?" I prompted, but he slapped a hand over my mouth and tipped my head back, and the view made me swallow my protestations.

"You don't get stars like that in the city, do you?"

I swallowed past the lump in my throat and relaxed into the blankets. "No, you don't."

"I would have dragged your ass to the treehouse, but I

figured the freshmen fifteen you put on might take the place down."

"You're such an ass, Liam," I said, but I leaned my head against his arm as we settled into the pillows. Surrounded by the sounds and scents of days gone by, it made it easier for me to digest all the mistakes I'd made when they were so far away —which was exactly his intention, I realized.

"I thought my attempts to cheer you up left a lot to be desired?"

"You know what I mean."

"Mom had mentioned she and Dad used to come out here and do stuff like this. I figured it was shit you girls got off on."

"How romantic," I teased with my heart in my throat.

"Shut up."

"Your mom didn't think it was weird we're going to stay out here?"

He grinned. "She thought it was sweet. Said she was gonna bug Dad to take her out dancing or something because they never do anything fun anymore."

"So, c'mon. What happened with your dad?"

Instead of answering, he pulled out another blanket and draped it over us. I tried not to think about how close we were. How our heat mingled together underneath the fabric. It'd be so easy to lean over.

"They're selling the land. The farm," he said after a while, breaking me from my fantasies. It was as effective as an ice bath.

"What?!"

His fingers pulled at a string on the blanket. "Yeah, dad told me when we were out fixing the tractor. There's some fancy big shot who wants to develop the land into a country retreat or some shit."

"He didn't give you a hard time about it, did he?"

I knew how much tension there was between the two of them. They tried to hide it, but men weren't as subtle about their emotions. They liked to think they were all stoic and that women were the emotional ones, but it was the other way around. I wanted to reach for him, but I stuffed my hands between my thighs to keep from doing it.

"Actually, he didn't...and that was somehow worse."

"We're a pair, aren't we?" I wasn't as good at lightening the mood, but he smiled anyway.

"Yeah we are. But enough about me. We came here for you. I don't want you to beat yourself up about what happened. Andrew's a grown man. You deserve better. When you find the right guy, you won't be running away from him. The right guy will make you want to stay put. Your mom left you, your dad died. Everyone you've ever loved leaves you. You're scared of having someone else do it, too. You think I've been here all these years and not noticed?"

"I—" my voice cut out and I had to turn away to keep from letting tears spill over my cheeks. How could he see straight to the heart of me so easily?

"Aw, fuck, Charlie. You know I hate it when you cry. I

take it all back." He tugged on my arm and pulled me close enough that he could wipe away my tears with the hem of his shirt. The familiar scent of his cologne wrapped around me on my next ragged inhale. I caught the barest glimpse of his abs which made all the emotion his words inspired clog inside my chest as a wave of heat swept over me.

Determined to ignore my response to him, I took several deep breaths to clear my head. "So you're saying I should have stayed with him?"

"Hell no." He sounded so offended I laughed. "If he was the right guy he wouldn't have let you go in the first place. If you did run, he would have chased after you."

"What about you?" If we had to talk about me any longer I'd go crazy. "I don't see you running down the aisle." It wasn't just a diversion, I was honestly curious. Even if I wasn't preoccupied with his mouth since the kiss, I knew he was attractive. There were enough girls always checking him out to clue me in if I'd been completely oblivious.

"I'm in no place to be in a relationship." I'd be lying if I said my heart didn't stop a little at his comment. But I was being silly. He was going to school, I was leaving. It'd never work. "Even if I could devote my time to her during vet school, I don't want to be in a serious relationship until I'm situated in my career and stable with a steady income."

"Is that why you rarely go on dates?" I asked.

"I date," he said and pinched my waist. I smacked his hands away, but snuggled closer to listen for the rest of his answer. I didn't even mean to do it, it was just habit. When he didn't push me away, I relaxed, listening to the way his words reverberated in his chest. "I just don't want to get serious yet."

I found his hand and took it in my own. His long, capable fingers were warm and callused as they cradled my smaller ones. "But things will never be just as you want them, Liam. My life is a testament to that. Just as you think things settle down and you have a good thing going, it throws you another curve ball. I survived my mom leaving, and then my dad got sick. I survived taking care of him, and then he died."

"You've seen how my parents can be sometimes," Liam said after a moment. "The stress, the arguments."

"They love each other," I insisted. "People argue."

"Sure they do, but it's not always enough. They've struggled my whole life putting food on the table. Providing for me and my sisters. I don't want a hard life like that for my family. I don't want to become my father, busting ass every day for a job that barely pays the bills and then having to sell it just to make ends meet. Besides, could you imagine me settling down? I can barely commit to listening to one song all the way through."

I laughed, then sobered. "Be serious."

He sighed and closed his eyes. "C'mon, Charlotte, you know I'm no good at this emotional shit."

"You always say that, but you know exactly how to make me feel better, so you must be good at *something*." Which wasn't a lie. After mom left and dad got sick, Liam was the only one who could deal when I finally broke from the strain. "And don't call me Charlotte," I added, though I knew it was pointless to remind him because in the years we'd been friends, he'd never listened.

"Well, you're pretty easy to cheer up. Cookies, a little time away. Piece of cake. Maybe I would kickass as the committed boyfriend."

I ignored the boyfriend comment. "You make everything seem so easy," I said as I lost myself in the deep blue-black endlessness of the night sky. "I wish I could be like you."

"Bullheaded?" he said with a laugh.

"To a point," I said honestly.

"You don't wanna be like me," he replied and tugged me closer to his warmth. My eyes began to flutter closed. I was warm, surrounded by Liam and felt safe. I always felt safe when I was around him and that was more important than any kiss. "You're perfect just the way you are."

CHAPTER SEVEN

LIAM

WE MUST HAVE FALLEN asleep in the back of my dad's old truck because when I cracked open my eyes what felt like seconds later, it was morning and I was fucking freezing, despite the blanket. Charlie had curled into a ball beside me, and at some point during the night, I'd wrapped myself around her to keep warm. I wished I could blame my baser human instincts for what happened next, but I'd be lying to myself if I tried.

Her forehead was braced on my chest and my nose was buried in her hair. At first, I didn't realize where the scent was coming from. I got excited thinking my mom was baking apple pie first thing in the morning until I remembered it was a Sunday and she was probably more interested in sleeping in than cooking.

Then Charlie shifted a little in her sleep and the green apple scent met my nose, nearly causing me to groan out loud.

Not that she would have noticed, as she was still snoring softly, her hands tucked in between our chests. But I certainly still wasn't asleep. Nope. Every single part of me had woken the hell up and was ready to go.

Head still cloudy with sleep, veins full of spiky adrenaline and the sweet, seductive call of lust, I didn't fully realize what I was doing at first. It's never been in my nature to curb my instincts and I've always been affectionate. So it didn't occur to me to resist the urge to pull her closer, pressing her soft curves to me. She shivered and made a little sound in her throat that I felt all the way down in my dick.

"Liam!" my grandma shouted from somewhere back in reality.

The sound of her voice was too close, and it jerked me so thoroughly back from the sex-fueled haze I'd been under that I threw myself backward, knocking my head on the toolbox and causing me to see stars.

"Fuck!"

I rolled to my side and away from making what could possibly be the biggest mistake of my life and was grateful for the pain spearing through my head. It kept me from thinking about how goddamn good she'd felt in my arms. It also quelled the raging morning wood.

But it didn't help the craving for her.

My whole body was still screaming that she fit so perfectly against me. I'd spent all weekend trying to forget the moment of insanity that had caused me to kiss her. Waking up wrapped in her brought back every second of how it felt to have her tight little body against mine. How, for just a split-second, she'd responded to me in a way that made me want to taste and take until we were both spent from it.

I forced myself to get up and slide down the tailgate. I waved to Grandma, who was on the back porch not too far from the barren field where I'd parked us for the night. She waved back and went inside the house, the screen door slapping shut behind her.

"Are you okay?"

The sound of Charlie's rusty morning voice had all of my muscles clenching down to keep from reaching for her and pulling her back against me. The groping, fumbling jerk wasn't what she needed right now. She'd opened up to me and I'd be damned if I'd be another Andrew who used her for what she was willing to give and then dropped her as soon as they were done. She meant more to me than that. It was just my dick who couldn't seem to get with the program.

Remembering that she was waiting on my answer, I composed myself long enough to nod and say, "Yeah, I'm fine. Just forgot where I was for a second, I guess."

"Did you have a nightmare?" I could tell from her tone she was smiling. Even though my head was pounding and I was mired between confusion and annoyance, I smiled back.

"No, I didn't have a nightmare, Charlotte. Grandma Dorothy scared the shit out of me." I pushed my fingers into my eyes, then rolled my shoulders.

"I can't believe we fell asleep out here," she said as she sat up. The blanket fell to her lap and my mouth watered at her rumpled state. It made me want to push her back against the blankets and kiss her 'till the sun was high in the sky.

"Me either." Though falling asleep in my truck was the least of my worries.

She began picking through her dark hair with one hand as she yawned. She didn't look any different, which confused me more than anything because when I looked at her, all I could think about was how much I wanted to see if there was anything else I'd missed about her over the past twelve years. I couldn't even count how many times she'd been close enough for me to catch the scent of her hair, but it had never hit me like it did this morning, and it only made me want to find out what other secrets she'd been hiding.

It must have been the kiss. Knowing what she tasted like, how she felt under my hands. It was driving me crazy wanting to do it again.

"What?" she asked, jerking me from my thoughts. "Do I have something on my face?"

She started rubbing at her cheeks. I cleared my throat and started cleaning up the blankets, folding them as though I had a clue how to fold shit. If I didn't keep my hands and mind busy, I was afraid I might do something really fucking stupid, like bury my face in her hair for another whiff of her shampoo.

"Nah," I said once I was certain I could control myself.

"Just need some coffee and a shower. Which do you want first?"

Charlie brightened at the mention of her addiction. "Coffee," she demanded. "Like you even have to ask."

She climbed over the side of the truck and reached out for me. I took her in my arms out of habit and helped her down. Minutes later we were pulling into the garage. A shower would help get my head on straight. Then we'd be driving back to campus and I'd have applications, deadlines, and papers to fill the spaces in my brain that were fixated on her.

"Don't even mention how short I am before I've had my first infusion."

I snorted, relieved to find that whatever the hell had happened this morning hadn't made shit even more awkward. As long as it never happened again, we'd be okay.

"Then I won't mention that you should come with your own footstool," I told her as I held the front door open for her.

"Not. Another. Word," she growled. Her nose twitched as she followed it to the happily bubbling coffee pot. She'd been to my parents' house so many times, she went right to the cabinet with the coffee cups, dove into the fridge for creamer, and sat herself at the kitchen table.

"I'll leave you to it and take the first shower then. Once you're sufficiently caffeinated you can have the next."

She waved me away as she snatched the fresh pot of coffee to fill her cup and I shook my head. She'd wouldn't be fully coherent until she had at least two cups in her, which would only serve in my favor.

I checked on Grandma Dorothy, who was happily clicking away at the TV as she crocheted a God-awful fluorescent orange blanket. "For your apartment," she announced cheerfully when she saw me standing in the doorway.

"I can't wait," I told her after pressing a kiss to the papery-thin skin of her cheek. "It looks awesome."

"I'll make one for Charlie, too. That girl is always cold. A woman shouldn't be living alone like that, I've said it before and I'll say it again. She needs a nice boy to look after her."

The reminder of her engagement to Andrew put a sour taste in my mouth. "Don't worry, Grandma. I take good care of her."

"Of course you do, dear," she said, then squealed. "*Wheel of Fortune*'s on. Spin that wheel!" I chuckled as I ascended the stairs to the bathroom, leaving Charlie to her caffeine fix and grandma to her t.v. shows and crocheting.

Twenty minutes under the warm spray hadn't been the best idea. The erection I'd tamed sprung back to life and I'd closed my eyes and wrapped my hand around my dick, trying and failing, not to think of her as I rubbed one out. The hot water cleared my head and jerking off at least kept me from fantasizing, but I doubted either would keep me sane for long.

It occurred to me as I got dressed that I was being a fucking chick about it. We got along. We had a good time. I was obviously attracted to her and based on the way she'd kissed me back, even if it was only for a second, she had to be at least a little attracted to me, too. Why couldn't we date? I'd spouted bullshit the night before, but Charlie wasn't just some one night stand. She was...Charlie.

The thought of asking her out made me nick myself as I was shaving. I cursed underneath my breath and tried to make myself see reason.

Just because I wanted to kiss the hell out of her didn't mean I should.

With that in mind, I finished shaving, but a call interrupted my thoughts. "Walsh," I answered.

"Liam, it's Matthew from the bar. Look I hate to do this, but you left me short Friday without notice."

My stomach sank, and my head filled with the memory of my bare kitchen cabinets and the stack of bills on my desk that I had due. "I know, I'm sorry. I had Tripp cover for me."

"I'm sorry, Liam, but I'm gonna have to let you go. There are a hundred other kids who'd kill to have your job. I need someone more reliable."

I sighed. I wanted to argue, but I could tell by the tone in his voice it would be no use. I'd simply have to find another job. Besides, it had been worth it to make sure Charlie was okay. I might have to survive on microwavable dinners for the next few weeks, but I'd make it work. "Alright, Matt, I understand. Thanks for letting me know."

After hanging up with my former boss, I found Charlie in the kitchen, watching my parents cook breakfast. I paused in the doorway as I observed her studying them. The naked longing on her face punched me in the gut and obliterated any lingering traces of disappointment from getting fired. I'd known her parents for most of my life, and when her mom left and her dad died, it was the first time someone I knew had passed away. It didn't compare to what she went through, but I knew I'd do anything I could to take away her pain.

Even if it'd put my future in jeopardy.

My mother turned and smiled. "Just in time for breakfast."

"As if that's something new," Dad said.

"Something smells good," I told her.

"Charlie said you two were outside all night watching the stars like we used to." She turned to my dad and narrowed her gaze. Then said, "I figured ya'll probably worked up an appetite."

Charlie eyed the plate of scrambled eggs, sausage, and toast my mother sat down in front of her. "You're a goddess, Mrs. Walsh."

My dad wrapped an arm around mom's waist and kissed her cheek. "That's what I try to tell her every day."

Mom bumped him with her hip, but she was blushing. "You both eat up now," she said to us, even though her eyes were on my dad the entire time.

They left together, my mom's giggles trailing behind. I shook my head as I sat down at the table across from Charlie.

"You'd think they were the ones in college instead of us," I said.

Charlie had thrown her hair up into a haphazard bun while I was in the shower. The sun shone in through the kitchen window and caught all the different colors, turning them into spun gold. It glinted in the light as she cocked her head to the side and sighed.

Without thinking, my mouth opened and I started to ask her if we could maybe take a chance. See where that kiss would take us.

Then she said, "I guess we better hit the road if we want to get back on time," and I lost my nerve. I had the drive back to campus to think about it.

Part of me already knew I was going to ask her. It was just a matter of getting up the balls to do it.

CHAPTER EIGHT

CHARLIE

I COULDN'T PUT my finger on it, but something was off with Liam. I chalked it up to the patchy sleep he must have gotten from snoozing outside in the truck and resolved to make it up to him the first chance I got. I really couldn't ask for a better friend. It was starting to wear on me how much I had to remind myself that's all he was, all he could be. What excuses I did have didn't seem to carry much weight anymore. Not when I spent the night wrapped in his arms. At first, I thought I'd been dreaming, but there was no denying how turned on I'd been when I'd woken up.

"Is everything okay?" I peered over at him since we were nearing our exit and he'd barely said more than one-word answers in response to my questions. "Is it about your parents having to sell the farm? I didn't want to push, but I'm here if you need to talk."

He scowled at the mention and I instantly regretted

bringing it up. "It's that and some...other things. It'll be alright, shortstack. I don't want you to worry about it."

"C'mon, don't go all strong and silent on me. Talk to me."

His scowl turned into a grin. "Since when did we become girlfriends? 'Cause I sure as hell don't talk like this with Tripp and Dash."

I rolled my eyes. "Don't deflect. I know something's bothering you." My left foot was already tucked under my right thigh, so it was merely a matter of twisting my upper body to direct all my attention to him.

"I don't know, Charlie. I didn't want the family business, you know that." I nodded, even though his eyes were on the long stretch of road in front of us. "But it's still where I grew up, it's all my sisters have ever known. I hate that I could have saved it if I hadn't been so determined to do my own shit."

"Don't say that. You can't sacrifice yourself for something your heart's not in. That's the difference between you and your dad. He gets up every day and works his ass off because he does love it. If you were to quit school and help him, you'd resent him and hate yourself within six months. That's no way to live." I lifted a shoulder. "Life is just too short."

He reached over and wrapped his hand around my knee, squeezed then released. I could feel the heat from his palm shoot straight to my belly. I swallowed hard.

"In my head, I get all that. I don't know, man."

"You hate to disappoint him."

"Yeah, I guess I still do," he said with a snort. "I guess some things you just never grow out of."

I nodded, but I didn't think that was all that was bothering him, but I didn't want to push too much. He'd tell me the rest when he wanted to. He always had. What I didn't want to do was smother him. He'd done enough this weekend, whisking me away when I needed space and time to regroup after the blowup with Andrew.

"I know you probably have work to catch up on or something. I texted the girls last night and they wanted to get together to bash men and have a drink. Would you mind dropping me off at The Georgetown on Tennessee?"

His head snapped over to me, his gaze intense. *Had I said something wrong?*

"You don't want to stop by your apartment?"

"If you don't mind leaving my stuff in the back of your truck, I'll get it after. Unless you want to leave it in my place on your way home?"

He was quiet for a few long seconds. Something else was definitely going on. Whatever it was, the mood inside the cab of the truck had gone electric. I shifted in the seat and pulled at the thin material of my jersey top.

Finally, he said, "If you're heading out, I can get some studying done at the library. I'll pick you up when you guys are done so you don't have to get an Uber."

"Are you sure?" I'd never wanted to back out of meeting my friends before, but they'd been begging for the low-down on what had happened with Andrew and I couldn't keep putting them off, despite how much I wanted this weekend with Liam to never end.

He gave me a look that said don't be crazy as we left the I-10 and began driving into the heart of town. In no time at all he was pulling into The Georgetown's parking lot.

For a moment it looked like he might ask me to stay, then he said, "Of course I'm sure. I can't keep you all the time, can I?" He said it lightly, but was there a hint of wistfulness in his tone or was that just wishful thinking on my part?

I spotted Layla and Ember by the entrance to the restaurant and sighed. I loved my friends, but all I wanted was my bed and maybe some ice cream. Wine would be a good substitute in the meantime, I decided. Lots and lots of wine.

"Call me when you're done and I'll come get you," he said as he came to a stop in front of the entrance.

"I will. Don't study to hard, Dr. Walsh." I hopped from the cab and turned to give him a smile.

"I like it when you call me that, Nurse St. James." He waved to Layla and Ember, who'd come up behind me. "Ladies," he said with a killer grin before driving off.

"Boy have you got some 'splaining to do," Ember said, and she tucked mine and Layla's arms into hers and marched us to the door. "But first, wine."

I couldn't argue with that.

Normally we'd all meet in Layla's apartment for a Tequila Tuesday game night, but this week we all had cramming to do for papers or tests and even though we'd been around the block a time or two none of us could risk failing. I followed the girls and the hostess through the dimly lit restaurant to a seat in the back. After taking our drink orders, a sangria for me, white wine for Layla, and a margarita for Ember, the waitress left us, and I almost called her back to saved me based on the way both of their stares honed in on me.

"What?" I said and resisted—barely—the urge to cross my arms over my chest.

They shared a look.

"Don't 'what' us," Ember said as he dark green eyes sparkled with attitude. Her dark red hair came to life in the wash of the flickering candlelight despite the messy topknot she wore it in. She was a knockout, but she didn't have time to fuss with it much considering she cared for her two younger siblings and still managed to save lives as an EMT.

Layla's beauty was quieter, subtler. Her dark hair fell in soft waves around her pixie face. She wore thin-framed glasses that accentuated her big blue eyes and despite her aversion to makeup, she was a dab hand with eyeliner. "Yeah, what the hell happened?" she asked.

I snatched one of the napkins from the dispenser and began ripping it to shreds. It wasn't the memory of what happened with Andrew that had me nervous. Honestly, he was barely a blip on my memory. It was Liam.

I don't know when it had happened, but he'd shifted from

a support role in my life to the leading man and I wasn't sure what to think of it.

"I thought he was going to propose—"

"What?!" They screeched simultaneously.

"Whoa, wait a second," Ember said, holding up a hand. "Rewind and start at the very beginning."

By the time I finished relaying what happened, we were on our second round of drinks. "And then, um, Liam got him to leave me alone and brought me back to Nassau so we could visit his parents for the weekend."

Layla leaned back in her seat and drank deeply from her glass. She gestured in my direction. "There's something you're not telling us. Did you want to say yes to his proposal?"

My head shot straight up. "*No!* Of course not."

"Then why are you on your fifth napkin?" Ember asked.

Shocked, I glanced down at my lap and found a veritable mountain of shredded paper. I forced myself to knot my hands on the table. "Look, it's not a big deal."

"I call bullshit," Layla said primly.

Ember nodded emphatically. "So do I. Spill."

"Well, Liam came up when Andrew was saying all these awful things," I had to take another long draw from my glass of sangria to keep from choking up. "Anyway, Liam was working that night and he must have heard or seen Andrew come up to me. The next thing I know, he's kissing me and then Andrew left."

"Whoa, whoa, whoa," Ember said. "Liam. *Liam* kissed you?"

"Wow," Layla added, adjusting her glasses. "I definitely didn't see that coming."

"You and me both."

"Then Lay, you may need to get your glasses checked because you're blind. They're perfect for each other."

I carefully gathered up the mess of napkins and rolling them in another to keep from spilling everywhere. "It doesn't matter. He just did it to get Andrew to go away. It didn't mean anything."

"Honey, a man doesn't kiss you and then take you on a weekend getaway if he doesn't want it to end up with more kissing," Ember said. She'd been in a relationship since high school, not a serial dater like I was or a dater-avoider like Layla, so we mostly deferred to her when it came to the opposite sex.

But she was wrong about this. "Not Liam. He didn't try anything else afterwards and we talked about it."

Layla jabbed her finger in my direction. "You're in complete denial, but we'll circle around to that." Her face fell and I reached for her hand on the table.

"What's wrong? Here I am blathering on and I haven't even asked how you guys have been."

"My *mother*. I can't believe I still let her get to me, but you know I've been applying to the internship at Thornhill? Well she called to tell me the other day if I insist on keeping my major in education that I can forget any financial assistance for senior year and not to even think about asking her for help with graduate school."

Layla's mom was a straight bitch. She was a living testament to why I never bothered looking for my own. Whereas mine abandoned me, hers never lets up. My phone rings, but I don't recognize the number, so I send it to voicemail and shift my attention back to Layla.

"Now you're the one who needs to listen. You don't need to live your life according to what she wants. She doesn't get a do-over. You deserve to be happy," I told her.

Layla took a deep drink from her wine and signaled for another. "I hear what you're saying, but that's a whole lot easier to say than to do."

"One step at a time, sweetheart. You have to cut those strings at some point," Ember said.

"And just when are you going to realize when you don't have to take care of your brothers and that it's your parent's job?" I asked Ember.

"Not up for discussion," Ember said. "Besides, my twin terrors are a hell of a lot less of a pain in the ass than Layla's mother and Liam put together."

I giggled and slurped down the rest of my third sangria. "Look who can dish it, but can't take it."

Layla was giggling, too, her cheeks flushed. "I think we've opened enough wounds for one Girl's Night."

"Yeah, but I always feel so much better after," Ember lifted her glass in a toast.

Layla and I touched ours to hers. "I'd say we should do it more often, but you two ladies drink too much," Layla said, then polished off her wine.

I did the same with my own. "Way too much," I said with faux graveness.

We were still laughing as we stepped out into the chilly night air. Their Uber was waiting by the entrance and I gave them a hug and helped them into the back seat.

"Text me when you get home, okay?" I said as I waited for them to buckle up.

"Yes, mom," they both said.

"You too," Ember added sternly, ever the mother hen.

"I will," I promised. I waved at their smiling faces in the back window as the Uber pulled away.

I may have had to concentrate extra hard on my way to the bench at the front of the restaurant. Remembering I promised to text Liam when I was done, I pulled out my phone and fumbled with the lock screen.

Me: I'm reaaaaddddyy.

It only took a few seconds for Liam to respond.

Liam: Omw

I wanted to think it was the sangria, but the delicious anxiety I felt had nothing to do with having too much to drink. It was Liam. All Liam. The cool breeze laden with the scent of grease from a burger joint nearby did little to combat the flush in my cheeks. I had to get a grip on myself before I did something stupid.

Like kiss *him* this time.

Talking myself out of my nerves wasn't helping, so I decided I needed to walk it off. As soon as I stood up, the blood seemed to drain from my head and I swooned, reaching out a hand to grip the back of the bench before I stumbled and fall face-first into the concrete.

But I didn't.

A hand gripped my arm, and I looked up to find Liam standing in front of me. I blinked a couple times to clear the blurriness from my vision. "Careful there, Charlotte," he said with a mile-wide grin. "Wouldn't want you to hurt your pretty face."

My belly flipped and I barely resisted the huge to lean into his grip. I managed to roll my eyes instead, which was a bad idea as it caused me to wobble in my heels. Then I narrowed them, because even with the three-inch assist, Liam was still ridiculously tall. "Don't call me Charlotte," I told the two of him. "You got here fast. You better not have been speeding."

"And you've been spending too much time with Ember, clearly. I didn't speed. I'd just gotten your text as I was leaving the library."

Because I wanted to step into his arms, I took one back. I controlled my wobbling by sheer will. "Let's just get out of here," I said, but it sounded a little desperate to my ringing ears.

"Done," he replied, and wrapped an arm around me to guide me out of the restaurant. When I stumbled, he pressed me more securely to his side. "Have a little too much to drink there, shortstack?"

"Just a couple glasses of wine. Don't judge."

He opened the door for me and kept me steady with one wide palm as I clambered up. "No judgement," he said, but I could clearly hear the smile in his voice. Instead of pissing me off, though, it made me want to laugh.

"You're such a good friend, Liam," I said as he buckled himself in. My eyelids were heavy and now that the rush of adrenaline was gone, I could feel myself starting to crash. Surrounded by the comforting scent of him, knowing I had nothing to worry about as long as he was there, I turned sideways in the seat and leaned over so I could lay my forehead against his shoulder.

He reached over and rested his palm on my thigh like I knew he would. "Any time."

I only meant to close my eyes for a second, but I must have dozed off, because when I opened them again, I found myself in Liam's arms. Blinking rapidly, I looked around and discovered we were in our apartment complex's elevator. Too emotionally and physically exhausted to move, I let my head drop back against his chest.

"Y'know, Charlie, after more than a decade of knowing

you, I should have known that a couple glasses of wine knocks you out."

I smiled against the material of his shirt and marveled how that it was even possible after the past few days. "I just want to take a shower, change into a pair of yoga pants and a T-shirt and eat a gallon of ice cream." I yawned and then tapped him on the shoulder. "You can put me down now."

He set me gingerly on my feet, his hands on my arms to steady me.

"I'm fine, I promise."

"You sure?" he asked as the elevator dinged.

"I promise. I don't think it can get any worse," I said with a laugh.

And then we stepped out into the hall and found nearly a dozen men in uniforms going in and out of the yawning door to my apartment.

CHAPTER NINE

LIAM

THE EASY, relaxed mood Charlie had been in since I'd picked her up from the restaurant disintegrated at the sight before us. Her shoulders tensed and her breathing grew shallow and sharp. My own gaze narrowed and I kept myself in check so I didn't go charging over demanding to know what the hell was going on. There'd been a ton of trucks in the parking lot and a whole mess of people congregated on the first floor, but I'd been too focused on Charlie to pay give any thought to why they were there.

Big mistake.

"Are you seeing what I'm seeing?" she asked and I kept my hand on her arm in case her knees gave out from under her again. Mostly it was for my own benefit. I needed to know she was okay.

"Yeah, what the fuck?" was all I could manage through gritted teeth.

Charlie inhaled and exhaled slowly, then she straightened her spine and marched across the hall to the disaster zone that was her apartment. She only wobbled a little on her heels until she came to a stop beside two middle-aged men in coveralls. After tapping one of them on the arm, she squared her shoulders.

"Excuse me. This is my apartment. What's going on?" she asked.

The two men turned to her and immediately their eyes went to the slight V of her neckline. I gritted my teeth and stepped up behind her. Catching my eye, they straightened their gazes, both turning red.

"Ma'am, your apartment flooded. We didn't find out until this evening because the space below yours is empty. The building manager had an emergency at another complex, so he'll be by in the morning to talk about your options. Until then, your apartment will be inaccessible."

She swayed in front of me, so I placed my hands on her shoulders. "F-flooded you said? But that's impossible. I haven't been here since Friday and there wasn't anything leaking at the time."

I thought back to Friday when Andrew had asked for her key to get his stuff from her place. Had he done this? Was he that spiteful? Then it hit me. If I hadn't given Andrew the key, she wouldn't be essentially homeless right now. This was entirely my fault.

"How long will it take to repair the damage?" I asked. I had to fix my mistake.

One of the guys, whose name tag read *Mac*, lifted a shoulder. "Four to six weeks depending on the severity. Once we clear it up a little bit, you can go in and assess your damages and gather any items you'd like." He pulled a business card from his breast pocket. "If you'll call the landlord's office tomorrow, they'll be available to go over your options."

"Options," she repeated.

"Hey, Mac!" came a shout from inside her apartment.

"Excuse me," Mac said, and disappeared inside.

Charlie turned, her eyes unfocused and her face devoid of expression. "Well, shit," she said after a minute of silence.

"Don't worry, we'll figure something out. But we should talk about this somewhere else."

"Somewhere else. I have nowhere to go." She barked out a laugh. "Have you looked inside there? It's a disaster zone, Liam."

"It's just stuff. It can be replaced." I guided her by the shoulders out of the melee while I figured out how to tell her what had happened. I'd tried to protect her and I'd wound up causing her even more damage.

For a few minutes we just watched the parade of repairmen go in and out. Each time they stomped over the sodden carpet, Charlie winced. As the minutes passed, her shoulders grew tighter and tighter until they were somewhere up around her ears.

"Why don't you stay at my place?" I said. I didn't know I was going to offer until the words spilled from my mouth. The more I thought about it, the more the idea made sense. It wasn't going to be forever. We were best friends, for fuck's sake. Of course she could bunk with me. It was my fault she was without a place. It was my responsibility to make it right.

"What?" She blinked owlishly up at me, like she was waking from a dream. "I'm sorry, what did you say?"

"Why don't you stay at my place until they've got yours sorted?"

She blinked again, her mouth hanging slightly open. Then she shook her head and said, "No, I couldn't do that to you. You love your apartment. We just talked about how you didn't' want to settle down and all that."

I shrugged, feeling awkward as hell. "It's not that big of a deal, and it's not like I'm asking you to marry me. It would just be for a couple weeks."

"I can't move in with you!" I wasn't sure her eyes could get any bigger.

I shot a pointed glance at the ruins of her apartment. "Well you sure as hell can't live here."

A variety of emotions crossed her face, starting with irritation and ending with resignation. "Just for tonight," she said after a while. "Just until I can talk to the super and figure out what my options are."

Our building manager had never been what you'd call responsible, so I didn't have any high hopes about her "options", but she'd already had enough shit dumped on her in the past couple of days, so I agreed. I waited outside her front door while they let her run in and grab a few things that weren't completely soaked. I would have offered to help her, but she had the wrinkle between her brows that meant she was looking to fight with someone.

As soon as she came out with a couple garbage bags full of her stuff, I took them from her hands and said, "C'mon, I know you're hungry. Let's heat up a pizza and I'll get you some medicine for the headache you've got."

She squinted at me. "How did you know I have a headache?"

After reaching the elevator, I turned to her and pressed the crease between her brow. "This right here."

She only sighed, and I figured I wouldn't push her for the rest of the night. She had enough to deal with. We loaded her things into my truck and he was silent for the short drive over to my squat little duplex. The paint on the clapboard siding needed refinishing. The door was a little cock-eyed and the landscaping was practically non-existent, but it was dry and it was as clean as a bachelor pad could get, which was a hell of a lot better than her place. And it'd save her more money than if she got a hotel.

I set her bags down underneath the kitchen bar as she kicked out of her shoes. While she threw herself on the couch with a grown, I grabbed a frozen pizza from the freezer, unwrapped it and set it on a cookie sheet while the oven preheated. I shook a couple Tylenol into my hand and brought them over to her, along with a glass of water.

"Take these."

She did as I'd instructed and gulped down the whole glass of water. "Thank you," she said on a heavy exhale. "I guess I'll know better than to think things couldn't get worse in the future."

I chugged my own glass of water, hoping the knot in my throat would dissolve. "I'm sorry, sweetheart, but we'll get it taken care of."

"I know. I just I hate it when things are out of my control." She frowned, and I couldn't help but laugh. "What?" she asked indignantly.

"You're gonna go through your whole life frustrated if you think you can control everything. If my family had taught me anything, it's that you have to learn to roll with the punches. Cliché, but it hasn't done me wrong yet."

She shook her head, then winced and slumped down against the couch. "I'd rather know what's happening. Have a plan. That way if something does go wrong, I'll know what to do."

"So, you're saying you should have planned to lose your apartment?" Maybe I was wrong about understanding this woman in particular. I scratched my head.

Tears thickened her voice and it froze me to the spot. Those tears were because of me. I'd done this to her as surely as fuck-stain. How I'd ever though I had a right to ask her for more was beyond me. "I should have had renter's insurance at least so that would have covered any possessions that are damaged so I could replace them. I should have had someone come over to check on the apartment while I was gone. If I hadn't been so distracted by what happened with Andrew, maybe this wouldn't have happened."

Guilt drew my eyes to the countertops. I could barely look at her. "Clearly you're still intoxicated because that's the biggest load of crap I've ever heard, and sometimes you can really be full of it."

"I don't want to argue with you tonight, Liam," she said with a sigh.

"I'm not arguing." I glanced over as the oven chimed and got up to put the pizza inside. "All I'm saying is you shouldn't be so hard on yourself. You can't control everything."

"I can try."

With the pizza in the oven, there was nothing else I could do to distract myself from telling her the truth. I braced my hands on the island and forced my gaze to her. God, she was gorgeous. Even sprawled across my couch, her face splotchy with the remnants of tears and her makeup faded, she was gorgeous. "Look, this wasn't your fault. If it was anyone's, it was mine."

She threw a hand over her eyes. "No, it wasn't. If anything, you're the only thing holding me together."

I flinched. "He flooded your apartment because of me."

"What?" she asked as she straightened, her red-rimmed eyes coming to me. "What are you talking about?"

"Friday after you broke up with him he came over to the bar asking for your spare key so he could get his stuff. I didn't even think about it because I was so pissed off from the things he said." I didn't even want to touch how scrambled my brain had been after kissing her. "I should have asked you if it was okay. I should have known he'd try something after the shit he pulled. I'm sorry, Char. Just tell me how I can make it up to you."

She wiped her face and took a shaky breath. "You gave him a k-key?"

I wished she'd yell. It would be so much easier than the heartbreak on her face. "Yes. I'm so sorry. If I could take it back I would."

Her shoulders slumped and she blew out a long breath. I braced my hands on the island, preparing for a thorough tongue-lashing. Bare feet appeared in my field of vision where they paused opposite the island. She was so close, but she'd never felt so far away.

"I don't know what to think about this right now," she began, then her voice cut off. I stared at her bare feet and realized she hadn't been able to get another pair of shoes. Because of me. "I don't want to be angry with you, I can't even remember the last time I truly didn't want to look at you. But that's how I feel. I'm tired. I'm overwhelmed. I'm homeless. It's too much. I'm going to go get a shower and get some sleep and maybe tomorrow I'll know how to handle everything, but right now, I think I need some space."

"I understand." My voice sounded like shit. I cleared my throat. "Do you need anything? Towels or—"

She shuffled her feet. "I can find them." Silence descended and I didn't dare break it. "Goodnight, Liam."

"'Night," I called to her retreating back. I wanted to say more, but I bit my tongue. She was right, she needed space. I'd done more than enough. I just hoped she could forgive me.

CHAPTER TEN

CHARLIE

MY CONFUSION HAUNTED MY DREAMS. Not only was I in an unfamiliar place, but the sense of losing all my things, of being displaced again brought back all the insecurities I felt after my mom left. I dreamt of her for the first time in nearly a decade that night. Every time I woke up in a cold sweat and tried to talk myself down until I passed out again, only for the cycle to continue on relentlessly. By the time the sun rose, I didn't feel any more rested than I had when I'd first put my head to a Liam-scented pillow.

I'd set several alarms the night before in five-minute increments and it took every single one of them to get me fully awake and out of bed in time for my clinical rounds at the crack of dawn. Luckily, I kept a couple changes of scrubs in my car so they weren't damaged and had grabbed them before coming to Liam's. I tossed them in his dryer as I padded around his place, trying not to make any noise.

I spent quite a bit of time in it since we'd left Nassau for Tallahassee to go to FSU, but I saw it with new eyes now that I'd be staying for God only knew how long. Unlike me, he hadn't moved around each year trying out new complexes and trying to find one that fit. He'd found this dinky little duplex our freshman year and had stubbornly stuck to it.

It was in a prime location just off of Lake Ella where we'd often jog together when our schedules matched. I'd point out the cute puppies and he'd patiently let me pet them or coo at the geese and ducks. But there'd be no jogging this morning. I wasn't sure I could look at Liam. He didn't have class until ten-thirty or work until five. Part of me wanted to see him peek out his door, but another was grateful he was still asleep. I didn't want to look at him and still be mad.

I pushed thoughts of jogging out of my mind and focused on getting ready. I didn't have any food here—I'd have to go shopping after clinicals and classes, another expense I couldn't really afford. Then I spotted the note on the counter. It was written on a flashcard in Liam's precise handwriting and propped against the coffeemaker.

Help yourself to anything you need. -Liam P.S. I'm a jerk.

Tears prickled the back of my eyes and then I gasped as the coffeemaker gurgled to life and began to drip hot, fresh coffee into the pot. The scent perked my groggy brain right up and it was ready and willing to forgive Liam all his transgressions. I hadn't had time to process everything, but coffee was always the way to my heart and he knew it. I filled a thermos from his cabinets and relented by taking a slightly overripe apple and a granola bar. His pantry was pathetically bear—men—and I decided I'd grocery shop that afternoon anyone. Who cared if I wouldn't have any money left? I'd need ice cream after I met with my building super this afternoon anyway.

The dryer beeped as I polished off my first cup of coffee and poured a second. I quickly dressed in my school-issued scrubs and packed a second plain pair to use for work afterward. I pulled back my hair into a serviceable ponytail and scrubbed my face with warm water and a hand towel. I made do with what little makeup I carried with me in my purse, a little concealer, some eyeliner and called it good.

I packed the snacks in my bag along with my change of scrubs and paused by the front door. I gave half a thought to waking Liam up, then I glanced at the clock. I wouldn't have time. Besides, I still wasn't sure what I wanted to say.

I DRAGGED myself into work after a long round of clinicals and an endless morning of classes. It was only the thermos of coffee I'd filched from Liam that kept me going. It didn't taste good after about the third reheat, but it kept my eyes open long enough to keep the patients I saw to alive and take notes during my lectures. The only negative was it constantly reminded me of him, what he'd done, that I'd see him in just a couple hours. I hated being on the outs with him. It felt unnatural.

He'd texted me once during the day, but I still hadn't replied. I was putting it off. The therapist who I'd been required to see after my mother's disappearance and my father's death told me I had an avoidant personality. I thought she was a quack at the time, but maybe she'd been onto something. I'd happily put off this confrontation, oh, *forever*.

Which is why I was at least looking forward to work. A lot of people looked down on elder care, but it soothed me. It reminded me of my dad's last days in hospice, of Grandma Dorothy and the good men and women who cared for them. I liked being that person for someone else's family. Eventually I'd like to go into critical care, but for now this paid the bills and gave me purpose.

"Good morning, Mr. Williams," I said as I pushed through the door to my favorite patient's room, but it was empty. I knocked on the attached bathroom door. "Mr. Williams?"

My heart began to thud dully in my chest. Had he left? Had he...passed away?

I couldn't bear the thought of it. I began to speed out the door when it pushed open and Mr. Williams, a thinly-built man with a shock of white hair and watery green eyes, lit up when he saw me.

"Charlotte!" he exclaimed and I smiled. He was the only person, after my dad, who I let call me by my real name.

"Mr. Williams. You scared me. I thought you'd left." I stepped into his embrace and inhaled the scent of Old Spice and antiseptic. My insides unclenched.

"You couldn't run me away, sweetheart. Who else would play chess with me and let me win?"

"No one," I said fondly as I got out the board and began setting up the pieces. "Did you take your medicine?"

He scowled, but we both knew it was only for show. "You should know better than to torture and old man."

I tutted at him and retrieved his medicine from the pharmacy station. "Bottom's up!" I said and his scowl deepened at my cheerfulness, but he complied. "Now let's see if I can beat you again."

"Not a chance, missy."

"Did you have a good weekend?" I asked as I carefully considered my opening move. It wouldn't matter what I did. Despite his age and my teasing, Mr. Williams was a shark at chess and I'd only ever beat him once and that was only because he'd just had surgery to repair his hip and had been on some serious pain killers. I chose a pawn at random and immediately regretted my decision when his beard twitched.

He mimicked my move, but I had no clue what he was planning. A chess genius I was not. "It was boring here without you to keep me company," he said. "What did you do?"

"I went to visit Liam's family near Jacksonville for the

weekend." I moved another pawn, but he struck and captured it with a masculine laugh.

I felt the tension leech from my shoulders the longer we played. I told him about Grandma Dorothy and her new fluorescent orange blanket. He had a similar one, this one an unearthly yellow, draped over the foot of his own bed. I even told him about the trouble with my apartment and how Liam had a hand in me losing it.

Mr. William's had three-quarters of my pieces by the end of my update. "Don't be too hard on him. He sounds like a good friend from what you've told me. He's probably madder at himself than you are at him."

I thought of the note he left me, the coffee he'd made. "I know that, but it just sucks all around."

"I know it does, but you can find another apartment. You won't be able to replace a friend so easily." With that sage advice, Mr. Williams moved his bishop and crowed, "Checkmate!"

I frowned at the board. "You're diabolical," I said, then began cleaning up the set.

"You're getting better. One day you may even beat me."

"Thank you, Mr. Williams, it's nice of you to say, but we both know I'm hopeless." I smiled at him and lifted the chess box in greeting. "Rematch next week."

"You got it," he said as he settled into his hospital bed and turned on the t.v. to the news. "You'll have to update me about you and your young man."

"We'll see," I said over my shoulder.

I finished my rounds with Mr. William's words fresh on my mind. I knew it wasn't Liam's fault for what happened, not really. Andrew had used the spare key a couple times before to get a spare set of scrubs for me when I was tied up in class or get something of his he left. It wasn't completely unreasonable for Liam to give him the key. After Andrew blew up at us...after the kiss...suffice it to say we were both distracted.

The girls weren't much help when I texted to let them know what was going on. They both lived in the same complex and had noticed all of the commotion that morning. I didn't get a chance to reply until I finished my shift.

Ember: OMG!!! That rat bastard! Do you need me to come over and help you clean up? I'll see what I can sneak in and salvage since they won't let you in. If you don't have a place to stay, you can crash here.

Layla: Tequila Tuesday at my apartment next week. Not optional! I'll even provide the tequila this time. Let us know what the super says or if we need to put a hit out on him.

I sent them both thank yous and promised to keep them updated. I didn't have a good feeling about my meeting with the super, but I headed there after work to get it over with. I'd feel better once I knew my options...I hoped.

I KNEW the meeting with the building manager wasn't going to go well when he had me wait for half an hour in the small lobby on the first floor of our apartment building. I never liked to linger there because it always smelled like spoiled milk despite the heavy rose-scented air freshener they had plugged in to every available outlet. By the time he called me back into his office, I was tired, nauseous, and ready to put my feet up after a long day of clinicals.

"Ms. St. James, thank you so much for your patience."

"Of course," I said as I took a seat opposite the ancient desk in the middle of the cramped office.

Despite the comfortable bed in Liam's spare room, I hadn't been able to close my eyes and turn off my brain. It was like everything that could go wrong, had. And I didn't get a good feeling about this meeting. I didn't know if it was left-over nerves from the day before or what, but there was a knot of tension in my stomach that no amount of chugging water would make go away.

Mr. Jergan, the building manager, was in his late forties or so with a shiny pink head and the remnants of hair he trimmed fastidiously around its rim. His mustache matched the salt and pepper of what hair remained and was trimmed razor straight. It twitched as he sifted through paperwork.

"I have some unfortunate news about your unit. It appears the sink in the bathroom had been blocked with a washcloth and overflowed all over the unit."

I swallowed around the lump in my throat and fought the

urge to cry in frustration. If he got away with this I was going to kill him with my bare hands. "I understand. An ex-boyfriend of mine used the spare key to get some belongings, or so he said. I never had any idea he'd do anything like this. I don't have renter's insurance, so he's cost me everything. Please, can you help me?"

His expression was unforgiving and my heart sank. "Seeing that the damage, though accidental, was at the hands of someone you're responsible for we're holding you liable for the damages. You're going to have to forfeit your deposit, you understand." His mustache twitched again and I focused on it as I considered my response.

"Sir, I can appreciate your position, but there has to be another apartment you can lease me in the meantime. If not here, then at some other building?"

"Currently, all of our units are full. Normally, we'd offer another for your use per the terms of your lease, but there are none available here or at another property. We will make our best effort to have the unit repaired in a timely fashion, but we won't be able to offer you accommodation in the meantime. I do apologize for the inconvenience. You're more than welcome to retrieve the rest of your belongings as soon as the maintenance crew has given me the all-clear."

Numb and disbelieving, all I could do was nod. 'Do you know how long it'll take for my apartment to be repaired?"

He leaned back in the seat and tapped his thumbs on the

armrests. "Hopefully within in the next two months, as long as the contractor stays on schedule."

It felt like the breath was knocked out of me. I couldn't afford a hotel for that length of time. Without the return on my deposit, I couldn't afford a first and last deposit either. Not without dipping into my overseas fund and I was reluctant to sacrifice my dream. But I'd have to if I couldn't figure out an alternative.

"If you'll sign and date these papers here, we'll get you all taken care of."

I glanced at the papers as he handed them over and decided I wasn't going to let him screw me. I took them and stood abruptly.

"Erm, Ms. St. James—"

"Thank you so much, Mr. Jergan. I'll give these a once over and return them to you once I've signed them. I hope you have a wonderful evening."

Without another word, I spun on my sensible white sneakers and marched out of his office and to the garage where I'd stored my car. I'd managed to use the bus to get it this morning before clinicals. Practically vibrating with frustration, I jabbed my key into the ignition and forced myself to drive carefully through the maddening evening traffic. College kids, liberal amounts of alcohol and unfettered free time did not mix well. Especially at a school like FSU with its notorious reputation for an epic social life.

I was still livid as I stalked through the grocery store by

Liam's duplex. I practically sprinted down the aisles loading my cart with comfort food. Aside from the brief respite of chess with Mr. Williams, it had been a hell of a day. I paid for the groceries and bundled them into the car.

Despite my pleas otherwise, traffic had cleared by the time I left the grocery store and I made it across town to the duplex in record time. Liam's truck was parked in the driveway and a light shone in the living room. I didn't want to be mad at him anymore, I decided. I missed my friend and it had only been a day. There was no more avoiding him.

I weighed down my arms with the bags because I'd rather lose circulation in my arms than have to go back for two trips. It was a stupid decision because it meant I didn't have a free hand to open the door. I sighed and kicked it with my foot and wondered if sleeping in one of the empty rooms at the adult care facility was an option. The last thing I wanted was for things to be awkward between us.

He came to the door without a shirt on and my tongue stuck to the roof of my mouth. He froze at the sight of me for a second, then took half of the bags in one of his hands causing his muscles to bulge. Needing to keep my distance from him was practically impossible now that we were living together.

"Thanks," I croaked and purposefully shifted out of the way and closed the front door behind me, the remainder grocery bags slapping against my leg along the way. I slumped against the wall with a frustrated growl, let the bags drop to the floor, and squeezed my eyes shut. Maybe if I clicked my heels together the world would go back to normal when I opened them again.

"Guess your meeting with good old Mr. Jergan didn't go very well." I heard the rustle of the bags as he carried them to the kitchen and then returned for the ones by my feet.

"You can say that again," I told him without opening my eyes. An epic headache started to beat a wicked tattoo in my temples. "Apparently because Andrew technically had access to my place because he had a key, his damage was my fault. So I'm out my apartment and a deposit. I don't exactly have a ton of money, so I'm pretty much screwed here because it'll take me forever to save up first and last month's rent for another place unless I dip into my overseas savings."

"That's fucked up," he said, and I was glad he didn't try to comfort me. One show of sympathy and I might have broken. "You know I can help you with the money, if you want."

But we both knew it was mostly kind gesture. Liam was a broke student saving for vet school like I'd been saving for my volunteer gig. I sighed. "I'm sure I'll figure something out."

I kept my eyes squeezed shut. Just a few more minutes. Maybe it was the headache, maybe it's because I didn't want to see him feeling sorry for me, but mostly it was not wanting to stare at him like a psycho.

"I wasn't kidding when I said I was a jerk," he said. "You wouldn't be in this position if it weren't for me. I can't say I'm sorry enough, but I can help you. You can stay here with me."

At that, I cracked open an eye. He'd taken everything out and had begun putting things away. "You can't be serious."

He leveled me with a look that clearly said how stupid he thought that statement was. "Of course I'm serious. If it makes you feel more comfortable, we can put a time limit on it. However long you think it would take you to save up money for first and last a new apartment. If you can forgive me that is. Even if you can't, you can stay here as long as you need to and I'll keep my distance, I swear."

It was the way he held himself apart that broke me. This is *Liam*. I knew he meant what he said. If I wanted to use his generosity to stay here and not talk to him again he'd let me. Because that's just who he was. I pushed off the wall and crossed to the kitchen where I wrapped my arms around him. "I forgive you. Please don't blame yourself anymore." I was aware of his bare skin beneath my cheek, the thump of his heart in my ear, but I tried to focus on him, on not fucking things up more than they already were. "I'm sorry for being pissed off. It was just too much."

His arms came around me and I felt his sigh of relief. "You don't ever have to apologize to me, Char. It was my fuck up. Just tell me we're okay."

"We're okay." I felt such relief in his arms that I knew I made the right decision. I could never stay mad at Liam for long anyway and I knew he'd never do anything like that intentionally. "I really don't want to put you out any more than I already have, but I have nowhere else to go right now."

"You aren't putting me out. I'm offering. Understand?" When I didn't answer right away he tipped my chin up with a finger and prompted, "The correct answer is 'yes, Liam'."

I tucked myself back against his skin. *Just one more minute.* "Are you so demanding and obnoxious with everyone or am I just lucky?"

I felt him smile against my hair as he leaned down and pulled me closer. "I save it all up just for you. Besides, you're not the only one in dire straits. My manager at the bar wasn't too thrilled with me this weekend. I got fired."

"What?!" I screeched. "Liam, no. You can't be serious."

"Don't worry, shortstack. Jobs like those are a dime a dozen, but it'll help me out to have you here for a bit while I look for another."

I pulled back to frown at him. "Well now I feel like a little shit for being upset yesterday. You have every right to be mad at me, too."

He shrugged and moved away to open the fridge for a beer. "Why don't we just call it even? You can have the spare room, we can split everything else and maybe we'll both get what we need. You get your overseas thing and I don't have to spend any of my college fund for vet school."

"Are you sure?" I asked.

"Don't worry, I plan on putting you to work." He threw himself on the couch and turned on the TV. "Cooking, cleaning. The usual."

Laughter bubbled out of me until he didn't join in. "What? Wait, are you serious?"

"Of course not. We'll split the rent and bills. Don't be a slob and we'll be fine. It's not like it's forever, Charlie."

Too exhausted to think of an alternative, I plopped down on the couch beside him and propped my head on a pillow against thigh as he flipped through shows on Netflix and sipped his beer. After selecting one, he began sifting his fingers through my hair until I purred in the back of my throat.

"That feels good," I said sleepily.

"Just relax for a while. Everything will work out."

Maybe everything had worked out for the best. It wouldn't be a good idea to act on my attraction to Liam now, not when we would have to spend the next few months together. If one of us caught hard feelings and things ended badly, I'd be forced to move again and I'd have to sacrifice the volunteer opportunity.

Not only that, but I'd risk my friendship with Liam. It might survive a failed relationship, but it'd certainly never be the same. I already worried it was fundamentally different because of one kiss. After almost losing him because of this crap with Andrew, I knew just how much it could hurt me and I knew first hand relationships weren't worth the risk. My own mother taught me that well enough. What I had with Liam was so much stronger...so much more important.

As he played with my hair and I drifted in and out to the

sounds of *Criminal Minds*, it was almost impossible to ignore how much I enjoyed him touching me, but I'd have to get used to being this close to him...and doing nothing about it.

If we were going to live together, anything more than just friends would have to be off limits.

CHAPTER ELEVEN

LIAM

THERE WAS something that looked suspiciously like break-fast waiting in a covered dish on the island.

This was impossible for three reasons:

1. I didn't have anything resembling cookware in my apartment (and probably hadn't since I'd moved in two years ago).

2. I wasn't sure anyone my age actually knew how to make food that didn't require a microwave.

3. The last time Charlie cooked something, we both wound up with food poisoning.

It wasn't until I spotted the takeout containers in the trash that I deemed the biscuits and gravy safe to eat and tossed them in the microwave to heat up as I got dressed. I didn't have class until eleven, but I liked to get up a couple hours early to hit the gym for a quick workout beforehand. I wolfed down the biscuits and gravy and shot off a quick text to thank

Charlie for the food. I felt a twinge of guilt that she not only stocked the cabinets and fridge the day before, but that she'd sprung for breakfast as well.

I hadn't been kidding when I asked her to move in. I'd been prepared to beg. Not only had I gotten fired from the bar, but bills were coming due and I'd been surviving on canned soup for longer than I'd cared to admit. This weekend at my parents was the first time I'd had anything home cooked since Christmas.

I could have asked my parents for help, but there was no way in hell I wanted to hear my dad bitch about how much money I was wasting living in a different city going after a useless education when I should have been helping him. The guilt and shame of having the gall to go to school when they were struggling was already overwhelming.

My phone rang as I jogged to my spot in the covered parking garage attached to our apartment complex. I answered it, breathing heavily. "Hello?"

"Willy, you forgot your good jacket at the house. You're gonna have to turn around and come pick it up so you don't catch a chill," came Grandma Dorothy's voice through the crackling line. She must be on the house phone. It had a lot of static on the connection. My parents didn't want to get rid of it because Grandma Dorothy liked to call her friends when she was of a mind to.

"Hey Grandma, it's Liam."

"Liam?" she asked, her voice breaking in the middle of my

name in a way that made me stop before I unlocked my truck and lean my head against the window. She'd always been the strongest person I'd ever known and to watch her deteriorate before my eyes was worse than if she'd been taken without warning like my grandfather had.

I swallowed back the choked feeling in my throat and told myself to stop being such a fucking pussy. "Yeah, Grandma, it's me. How are you doing?"

There was a lengthy pause as she sorted through the labyrinth her mind had become, but I was patient. Even though I'd been in a hurry to get to the gym, everything had ground to a halt when she called. If I'd learned nothing else from being friends with Charlie, it was that each moment with your loved ones was precious, and there wasn't a chance in hell I was gonna miss out on any of them.

"I'm doing fine, sugar. You should come by and see your grandma sometime. I sure do miss you."

I didn't remind her that she'd seen me just a couple days ago, but it still stung like a son-of-a-bitch that she didn't remember because I knew there'd come a day when she wouldn't remember me at all.

"I'll try to come up this weekend when school lets out. I promise."

She made a humming sound that was as much a part of my childhood as the taste of her sugar cookies. I urged myself to hold it together as she said, "How's school, honey? Are the other kids playing nice?"

Laughter burst free, but I choked it. I rubbed at my eyes. "It's going pretty well. Passing all my classes and the other kids are treating me just fine."

"Good. That's good to hear. You'd tell me if someone was bullying you, right? I won't have none of that nonsense with my grandson. You hear me?"

"Yes, ma'am," I said obediently. I was reminded of all the times she'd been forced to discipline me for one harebrained scheme or another I'd concocted while under her care. For such a small woman, should could sure as hell be intimidating, even though I towered over her, both then and now.

"I'm glad you brought that Charlie over. I've been thinking about her. She seemed upset, though. Is everything okay?"

I thought of Andrew and considered, not for the first time, what I'd like to do to his ass if I saw him again. "She and her boyfriend broke up, so she's having a bit of a rough time."

Grandma hummed again. "That poor girl. I'm glad you brought her by, then. People need to be around family when they're hurting, and I've always considered Charlie to be part of our family."

"She feels the same way," I said.

"Alright now, I think it's about time I put on my stories. You call me tomorrow, okay, honey?" For as long as I can remember, Grandma Dorothy could be found watching her soap operas from morning to afternoon. It was good that some things hadn't changed. Yet. "Here's your mom, she'd like to talk to you."

"Okay, Grandma. I love you." I used to feel awkward saying it. My whole family loved to say "I love you". It didn't matter the reason or occasion. There was always a chorus of them when we got together. I didn't get it until the day I visited Grandma in the hospital for the first time and realized she might never hear me say it again. Ever since then, I've made it a point to say it every chance I got.

"Love you, baby doll. I'll talk at you later."

"Later," I said with a laugh.

"Liam?" Mom said as she fumbled with the phone.

"Hey, Mom, what's up?" It had to be important if she was calling the day after I saw her.

"Sorry about that, honey. Your grandma hasn't been feeling well lately and she's been antsy all night wanting to talk to you."

"That's alright, mom. You don't have to apologize. I wish I could help out more, but I couldn't miss anymore classes this semester."

"Don't you think on that for a minute. We were glad to see you. I was going to talk to you about everything this weekend, but Charlie seemed upset and I didn't want to intrude."

My stomach dropped. "What is it?"

"Your father mentioned he told you about the plan to sell the land?"

"Yeah, he did. I hated to hear that, mom. I wish there was something we could do."

"Well, there was a reason why."

"What is it?"

"It's Grandma Dorothy, honey. Her doctors tell us she's in a rapid decline. She needs to be hospitalized soon, for her health and safety. We do our best, but she needs more care than we can provide at home. It's one of the reasons we're selling. It's the only way we'd be able to afford for her care."

Guilt twisted at my heart. "Are they sure?"

Mom sighed over the line. "They're sure. I just wanted to let you know. Your dad was going to tell you, too, but it's been really hard on him. He may seem hard, but he has a big heart."

"Thank you for letting me know. Keep me updated, okay?"

"Of course. You call me if you need anything, won't you?"

I managed to say goodbye before I lost it.

"YOU LOOK WORSE than I did yesterday," Charlie said as soon as I stepped in the door.

I grunted in answer and dropped my bag of school shit by the front door and toed off my shoes, leaving them by my bag. After a brutal morning at the gym where I tried to erase the conversation with Mom from my brain and an even longer afternoon of classes I was beat. None of the applications I'd submitted the night before had returned any results and I had another stack of overdue notices crammed in along with my textbooks and dirty gym socks.

"Well, hello to you, too," I said.

"Everything okay?"

I snorted. "Yeah, sure."

"I ordered pizza," she said with false cheerfulness.

At her hollow tone, I grimaced. I was being a dick. "Charlie..."

"I got you the cheese and mushroom you like," she interrupted.

"You don't have to take care of me, Charlie. Breakfast and now pizza. You don't have to be weird about living here."

"I'm not being weird. I'm trying to be nice," she said as she pulled out paper plates. The scent of cheese and tomato sauce filled the air, reminding me I'd stupidly skipping lunch after the gym. Well, skipped is a strong word. *Didn't have the money for* would be more accurate.

"Didn't we already have a conversation about being nice?"

She rolled her eyes. "Let's not go there."

"Sorry. It's just...it hasn't been a very good day." I scrubbed a hand over my face. *That was the understatement of the year.*

Charlie loaded up the plate with a gargantuan sized pizza from Momo's, a local legend for pizza slices bigger than your head. "Well, I'm here and I have ears if you want to tell me what's got you looking like you're going to incinerate innocent civilians with your eyesight."

I tore into the pizza still standing and said, "I'm never letting you watch *X-men* again."

She took a bite of her own, licked the sauce off her lip. I cursed myself for the thin athletic shorts I was wearing and casually slid onto a stool at the island so she couldn't see the outline of my dick through them.

"Seriously, though. What's wrong?"

"Mom called me today."

Charlie set the pizza on a paper plate. "What is it?"

She'd gone completely white. "Shit, Char. This is why I didn't want to tell you."

"Is it your parents? Grandma Dorothy?"

The knot in my stomach hadn't dulled with an hour in the gym. It intensified under Charlie's agonized expression. I swallowed a bite of pizza, but it was a struggle. "Grandma isn't doing so hot. They had to put her in a home. It's why they're selling."

"God, Liam, I'm so sorry.

I stood, suddenly unable to sit here with her soft brown eyes looking up at me. It made me want to hold her, comfort her. Those things were alright before, but hell if I understood why they made me so damn irritable now. I couldn't deal with any of it. I didn't want to. "I'm gonna grab us a six pack to go with this pizza."

She took a step back, dropped her hands When she spoke, her voice was tentative and I immediately felt like a dick. "That sounds great. We can have another movie night and veg out, okay?"

"I'll be right back," I told her.

The short run to the convenience store down the road allowed me to put a lid on my bullshit. She had enough on her plate without dealing with me. I'd find another job and she'd go off to wherever and things would get back to normal. They had to. By the time I got back to the apartment, I had that lid screwed on so tight I practically vibrated with it. Sitting next to her on the couch was like torture.

"Thanks for the pizza," I told her after the movie, getting to my feet almost before the credits rolled. "Even if you're still fucking weird for not liking mushrooms."

She pulled a face as she picked up our empty bottles and rinsed them. "They're so gross. I still don't see how you eat them."

I licked my lips. "Mmm-mmm, good," I said.

She laughed and slapped at my shoulder. "Do you mind if I take the first shower? It's been kind of a long day."

"No, go right ahead. I've got some studying to do anyway."

With a nod and a small smile, she turned around, then paused and turned back. "I'm here if you need me, Liam."

I lifted a shoulder. "Thanks."

"I'm serious. You were there for me. I want to be there for you, too," she said.

"You don't owe me anything, Charlie."

"Of course I do," she said, then disappeared into the bathroom.

I heard the shower turn on a minute later, and I took my books into my room, turning on the light beside my bed before throwing myself onto the mattress. Five minutes turned into ten, and I realized I couldn't remember a word of what I'd read. I shrugged my shoulders, figuring it was because I wasn't used to having someone else in the apartment. After nearly four years of living by myself, I'd kind of gotten used to it, even though I'd spent most of my life crammed in a house with my brothers and sisters.

The truth was, I'd never had a woman stay the night at my place before.

Charlie would hang out, but sleepovers had never been our thing.

Now I realized why.

I slammed the book closed, tossed it on the floor, and relaxed back onto my pillows. I couldn't seem to focus, couldn't get rid of the tension in my shoulders. It was probably because of my parents and bills.

As my thoughts drifted, I found them going to the shower, to Charlie. For a second, it occurred to me that she was naked in the house with me. I stumbled to my feet and stubbed my toe on the book. I muttered curses and kicked the book across the room. Limping, I turned in a circle and considered going back to the gym for another workout, then rejected the idea.

Instead, I hobbled to the door, pulled on my shoes with a muttered curse and went out for a jog. Everything was going to shit and all I could think about was what my best friend looked like naked.

CHAPTER TWELVE

CHARLIE

THE BLARE of my alarm woke me from a dream, a moan still clinging to my lips. My cheeks were flushed, my thighs clenched, and my hands twisted in the mangled remains of my sheets. My ears rang, but it wasn't from the drone of the alarm. I'd been holding my breath and it came out in one long exhalation, lungs burning with the effort to draw new air in. Spots studded my vision.

"Jesus Christ," I managed as I sat up, carefully releasing my strangle-hold on the sheets.

With numb hands, I fumbled with my touch screen until I silenced the alarm. But it wasn't the sound replaying in my brain. It was the sound of Liam's groans echoing in my ear from the sordid dream I'd been torn from.

This was bad.

I covered my face with a pillow hoping to drown out the memory of his hands on my skin, his filthy words in my ear, but I couldn't. The door had been opened weeks ago when he'd kissed me and there was no amount of locks that would keep it closed. No amount of forgetting could wipe away the memory when he was on the other side of a thin wall, refreshing it day in and day out. Especially not if I was going to start having wet dreams with him in them.

We'd been living together nearly a month now and I'd thought everything was going to be fine...apparently my body and brain had other ideas.

I rubbed my thighs against each other in an effort to sate the aching emptiness between them, but there was no quenching it. Sex with Andrew and I had been sporadic at best and before we broke it off, we'd been in a bit of a dry spell. I dipped my fingers between my legs and stifled a moan. There was no doubt that the dry spell was over.

It should have embarrassed me to realize Liam was the reason, but I was too turned on to think of anything but finishing what the dream had started.

As I was rubbing furiously, my lip clamped between my teeth, I heard the tell-tale sound of Liam's door opening and his feet padding against the creaky wooden floor outside my door. Oh, God, I knew I should have stopped, I knew I should have pushed all thoughts of him, and that kiss, out of my mind, but the forbidden aspect, the thrill of knowing he was on the other side of the door made the walls of my pussy clamp around my fingers in vicious delight.

I tensed my stomach and held my breath hoping to force

the orgasm before I truly fucked up and let him know what I was doing. The mere thought of having him burst through the door and catching me in the act had my fingers quickening their pace. Sounds were coming from the bathroom now, right across from my room. The light shone in the thin space underneath my door. His shadow danced across the floor inches from where I lay in bed touching myself to the thought of him.

My chest burned for air and I gasped, sucking it in as quietly as possible when I could hold it no longer. His shadow paused and I nearly squeaked in surprise. Even though shame burned in my stomach it was no match for the rising undulation of pleasure. My free hand dove under my shirt and cupped the swollen weights of my breasts, my nipples already hard and aching against the flat of my palm.

Water splashed in the sink and I recall the many showers I'd taken in the three weeks since I'd been living in Liam's duplex. I'd done my level best to think of anything but the fact that he was on the other side of the door while I was naked. As my fingers dipped into my wetness I couldn't think of anything else. He'd been the one to kiss me. Had he been thinking of me like this too?

Heat covered my whole body.

Had Liam been touching himself like this to thoughts of me?

Maybe another person would have been turned off by the thought, but it only made me bite my lip hard enough to taste the copper tinge of blood. I sucked away the sting and arched my neck as my hips began to roll.

He had no idea I was awake, let alone what I was doing, but that didn't make it right.

In fact, it probably made it worse.

Sharing his place with me was a show of trust. That he could trust me not to snoop, not to be a dirty Peeping Tom as his new roommate. I was his friend, and by taking advantage of the little sliver of invitation, I was betraying our friendship. But dammit, a nuclear bomb couldn't have stopped me from shifting to thrust my fingers inside and imagining they were his. Oh God. I'd never be able to think of his hands without wanting them inside me again.

This was such a bad idea, but I couldn't stop.

The faucet turned off in the bathroom and I swore he could hear my heart beating right through the door it was so loud. I tried to swallow, but my mouth was so dry, it was impossible. Did he do something to the heat? He must have, because my clothes were sticking to my skin and I was about two seconds away from having a heat stroke. Could that happen in the middle of March?

His footsteps drew closer to my room and I felt everything inside of me reaching a fever pitch. A knock came at the door and a desperate cry hovered on the edge of my lips. He knocked again and knowing he was there pushed me right over the edge. I turned my face to the side and allowed a soundless cry to escape into one of the pillows he'd given me that still smelled of him.

"Charlie?"

The crest overtook me a second time at the sound of his voice and I shuddered in silence, my thoughts fractured and conflicted. My alarm blared again, a sharp splinter of light in the fog of pleasure. I slapped a hand on it with a muffled shriek.

"You awake in there?" Liam called as the alarm cut off.

A shaky breath rattled free from my lips and I sat up in bed, pulling the sheets up as far as they would go. "Yeah, I'm up." I hoped my voice didn't sound as warbled and breathless as I thought.

A thud came from the other side of the door. I pressed my back into the headboard and gulped in deep breaths.

"You mind if I come in real quick?" he said through the door.

Mind? I wondered desperately if he'd be able to scent my orgasm the second he opened the door. Would he see it on my face? I had to hope not.

I frantically straightened the comforter and hoped it said restless sleeper rather than recently masturbated about its occupant. "Come in!"

The way the room was situated, the door opened right to the dresser and I spotted Liam's reflection in the mirror above before he pushed all the way through. In it was a half-naked body. Liam's half-naked body.

This is wrong, I told myself as the aftershocks danced along my nerve endings. So, so, so wrong.

The reflection in the mirror turned, offering me a delectable profile view. It really wasn't fair how good-looking he was. It was unnatural, I decided. Even so, I couldn't tear my eyes away.

The verdict was in. I was a terrible person. Because no one should look at a friend the way I was looking at him.

He leaned around the open door and I forced my gaze up to his eyes. "What's up?" I asked.

"I just wanted to let you know I got a call back for a job a different restaurant, so I won't be back for a couple hours. If they hire me, I may start work tonight."

My lips twisted into what I hoped resembled a smile. "That's wonderful! I'm so happy for you."

I knew how hard he'd been looking for a job to replace his bartending gig. I felt wholly responsible for him getting fired. The past couple weeks I made it a point to help him scour the local listings and helped him beef up his resume to atone.

"Thanks, I..."

His eyes left mine and traveled down the length of my body encased by the comforter. "How are you not burning up? It's like a furnace in here."

I chuckled nervously. "Oh, it's nothing. I must have gotten cold."

Was it my imagination or were his eyes boring holes into the fabric?

"Was there something else?" I asked. The sooner I could get him out of my room, the sooner I could take my own shower and wash this whole morning away. With his eyes on me and the memory of the orgasm still dancing along my skin it was almost too much.

I was too close to asking him to stay.

Too close to taking another kiss.

Too close to wondering what it'd feel like to have his hands bring me to the edge instead of my own.

"I'm done in the bathroom if you need to use it."

My cheeks reddened as the image of having him in there with me surfaced. Get it under control, Charlie. "Thanks, I'll be out in a minute."

He shifted, pausing in the doorway for another tantalizing second, then turned and left me with the image of his ass framed in a thin cotton towel seared into my brain.

I didn't get out from under the covers until I was heard his bedroom door shut behind him, then I sprang into action, grabbing whichever clothes were closest and my phone, then zipping to the bathroom. My muscles didn't relax until the bathroom door was also shut between us. I stripped down, my whole body tingled with awareness. I needed a cold shower immediately.

My phone rang as I was stepping into the shower, but I didn't recognize the number, *again*, so I ignored it and forced myself under the frigid spray instead. As I soaped up, I slowly turned on the hot water until I was no longer shivering. By the time I finished washing and conditioning my hair, I could breathe normally again. After I exfoliated and shaved, my thoughts settled. When I stepped out to towel off and lotion up, I was convinced I could handle seeing Liam again and not think about the dream, my fantasy, or what he looked like in that towel.

That is, until I got dressed and nearly bumped into him in the hallway and then backed up so quickly I collided with the wall.

Dressed in crisp black slacks and a long sleeved button-down shirt, he was as mouth-watering as he had been in the towel. I couldn't decide which version of him I liked better. It wasn't fair he looked as good fully dressed as he did half-naked.

"Jesus, Char. You okay?"

I rubbed the back of my head. "I'm fine," I said to the notch at his throat. His heartbeat fluttered there and my first thought was that I wanted to kiss him there, right where his scent was strongest. "I'm fine."

"You sure?"

"Yeap." I spun around and marched to the kitchen where I pulled out the makings for cereal. "You want some?"

He sat down at a stool by the island. "Sure. Thanks. Are you sure you're okay? You've been acting...weird this morning."

I busied myself with the bowls. "Yeah, I'm fine. Just an early morning."

He chuckled. "It's nearly eleven."

My glare didn't incinerate him like I'd hoped as I handed him his cereal. "Eat your food," I ordered, then began smashing buttons on the Keurig hoping at least one thing would go right.

"Stop, stop," Liam said, as he got to his feet and put his hand over mine on the machine. "You're going to break it like that."

All I could do was growl.

"Go sit down," he said with a laugh.

I took my seat next to his and stuffed my face with cereal so I wouldn't do something stupid like ask him to kiss me again.

CHAPTER THIRTEEN

LIAM

FOR THE FIRST time in all the years that Charlie and I had been friends, things were fucking awkward and I didn't know what to do to fix them. In any other situation, I'd know what to do to dispel the tension. If she were any other girl, I'd be able to bullshit my way out of any circumstance. But this was Charlie and none of my moves seem remotely appropriate.

Each day since she'd moved in had been pure torture.

Not that she wasn't a great roommate. She was reasonably clean, quiet, and at some point, had learned to cook like she'd been doing it for years. Hell, under any other circumstances, I'd be asking her to room with me for the foreseeable future, but that wasn't what was driving me crazy.

It was all the things I'd never noticed before because I'd framed her as a friend and nothing more. It was all the things

I'd conveniently forgotten because she was "one of the guys" instead of one hundred percent woman.

But now I couldn't escape them.

Things like I realized she never wears a bra when she goes to sleep. Now, we're both sitting at the island pretending to eat cold cereal and looking at our phones, except I can't focus on anything but the way her shirt is hugging her breasts and how I'm dying to know what she's hiding underneath it. I shifted in my seat and gulped down my soggy cereal, but no amount of distasteful visualizations can undo the reality of her oh-so-delectable body sitting across from me.

When I managed to pull my eyes away from her tits, I realized she'd been watching me, and I clear my throat. "I'm sorry, what?" I'm such a tool.

"I said, what time is your interview?"

How had I never noticed her lips before? They were slightly top-heavy and the most delicious shade of pink. Last night she'd made pasta for me and she'd licked away some sauce from her bottom lip. I'd nearly lost my ever-loving mind. With any other woman, I would have pushed her back against the refrigerator and taken that mouth. I would have had my hands everywhere on her body, anywhere they could reach. With any other woman, I would have slipped her little pajama shorts down over her hips and thrown one of her legs over my shoulders to feast on what I was really craving.

It didn't help that I was 99.9% certain I'd nearly caught her playing with herself this morning.

In that one moment I'd nearly taken back all the promises I'd made myself about keeping my distance. I'd weathered the nights with her a few feet away in those frequent showers. It nearly killed me going for a run every time she took one, but I made it work. The mantra that we'd only need to live together for three more months is what kept me going.

Then, I'd stepped into her room and seen her red-faced and hiding underneath the comforter. At first, I thought she hadn't been feeling good. I'd almost offered to get her, I don't know, some soup or some shit. Then, I realized she couldn't meet my eyes. I'd barely been able to speak, let alone keep my dick from tenting the towel I'd stupidly worn to talk to her. I don't even remember what I'd said, but I do remember catching the scent of her arousal. It was burned into my brain.

Despite all the voices in my head telling me it would be a mistake, it was hard to listen to reason when my whole body was screaming yes.

She snapped her fingers in front of my face. "Liam? Hellooo? Did you study too hard last night, or what?"

"Yeah," I managed to say, then dumped the rest of my breakfast. There was no way I was going to be able to focus on anything other than what was going on beneath her sexy-as-hell pajamas. Christ, she was driving me insane. "I mean, I must have."

I'd braced my hands on the sink as I tried to control my reaction without looking like an idiot or coming off as a jerk for staring at her body. God knows I didn't need to be just as much of a dick as her ex. I was supposed to be the person she could trust not to be an asshole. Not the guy who took advantage of her when she was vulnerable. This was Charlie. I shouldn't have to remind myself, but I did. I repeated her name over and over in my mind. Tried to remember all the times I considered her to be one of the guys.

Her chair scraped against the linoleum floor and her feet padded toward me. The warmth of her hit my back, followed by a soft cloud of that fucking green apple shampoo. I was going to have to find every bottle of it and hoard them when she left.

Then it hit me. She was leaving. It wouldn't be now, but in a few months she'd be hundreds of miles away doing God-only-knew what and I wouldn't get these early mornings with her.

"Is everything okay?" she asked from behind me.

Her voice was smoky with sleep and sexy as hell. I wanted to hear her screaming for me in that voice. Pleading in it. Then I wanted to make her breathless until she couldn't speak at all.

My hands fisted on the counter and I straightened without turning to run cool water from the sink and splash it on my face. "Yeah. Yeah, everything's fine."

Everything was not *fine.* I was about ten seconds away from doing something I'd regret. Like taking her back to her bed, *my* bed, and giving her a round two that'd have her seeing stars.

"You sure? You don't sound so good. Are you getting sick? I could run you to the clinic. Of course, I'm almost an official nurse. I could probably give you an exam right now." She wiggled her eyebrows at me. Normally I'd give as good as I got, but if I wasn't on fire before, the thought of her stripping me down and playing doctor sure pushed me over the edge.

I shoved away from the sink, keeping my back to her. "I'm fine, Charlotte." My tone was too harsh to be teasing.

"Don't call me Charlotte just because you're in a pissy mood," she said to my back. I knew if I turned around I'd find her with a hand on her hip and her eyes shooting fire. It was almost worse than seeing her all soft and sleepy.

Keep walking Walsh.

"I'm not in a pissy mood."

"Could've fooled me! If you have a problem with me living here, just man up and say so. You don't have to be a dick about it."

I sighed heavily as I enter my bedroom. "Look, I'm just in a shit mood, that's all. It has nothing to do with you."

"Are you sure?" she asked, following behind me and plopping down on my bed, which I was determined to ignore. I'd already spent too much time imagining her there. I didn't need the reality right in my face. "Because ever since I moved in you've been acting really weird. If I did something, just tell me. This is exactly why I didn't want to move in with you in the first place."

I could only hope I got the job and started tonight. The

less time I had to spend at home with her, the better. At the very least I hoped working long hours would make me too exhausted to get horny, but who was I kidding. It didn't take much for me to get turned on around Charlie these days. "I'm sorry. I promise you haven't done anything wrong. I like having you here. To be honest, I probably get more from it than you do. You've been a great roommate. And friend." I had to keep reminding myself of that.

"Then what the hell is going on? You can't even look me in the eye anymore." She put an arm on my bicep and turned me to face her. Staring into her gaze "Please, Liam. Whatever it is, I can help. I don't want to make you feel like a guest in your own home, and besides, we're supposed to be able to talk to each other. So talk to me."

But that was the problem.

The last thing I wanted to do was *talk*.

"There's nothing to talk about. I've got that interview and I need to head out soon. Do you need anything before I go?"

Her mouth twisted and she took a step closer, pressing me against my dresser so I couldn't escape. The closer she got the less oxygen there seemed to be. My heart began to race like I'd run a couple miles.

"You're really not going to talk to me?" She sounded hurt, which didn't help my self-control. "Since when do we do the silent treatment?"

I shoved out from under her touch, unable to stand the feeling of her hands on me and turned to walk away. The destination didn't matter, the only thing that did was getting away from her until I could remember all the reasons I'd been repeating to myself for the past few weeks.

We both needed to save money by sharing the house.

Sex would only complicate both of our lives.

We were friends.

Then she reached out a hand and took mine. Heat shot up from the contact and I'd never known there was a temperature hot enough to freeze, but that's what it did. Her touch froze me down to the core, stopping me in place. No amount of reason could have spurred made me leave when her hands were on me.

I turned, my whole body tense with indecision.

Her brows furrowed and her hair was a wild mess around her face. She bit her lip, sucked it into her mouth.

Fuck just friends. Then took a step toward her, come what may. *We could be so much more than that.*

My hand tightened on hers, then tugged, reeling her in. She glanced down at where I held her and her mouth opened into a little O of surprise. I liked my own lips in anticipation. That mouth. God, I wanted that mouth.

"Liam?" she asked, her voice quavering. "What are you doing?"

I crowded her into the dresser where she'd had me pinned just moments before. Her expression wasn't confused anymore. And she wasn't nervous like she'd been the first time we'd kissed. Some part of me recognized the flare of arousal in her eyes, the same part that had made the split decision to kiss her in the first place.

"I changed my mind."

She squeaked out a sound of surprise when her back came in contact with the dresser and her hands grappled for a hold, but slipped once before she could steady herself. "A-about what?"

I bracketed arms around her and smiled a little at the way her breath caught at my closeness. I liked her nerves. I liked having her off balance. "This kiss. What if it wasn't a one-time deal?"

Before she could respond, I dipped my head and nuzzled into the curve of neck and shoulder. I didn't kiss her there, not yet. The last time had been rushed. If I was going to hell for this, I was going to take my time about it.

"But I thought you said—"

"Forget what I said." My lips were close enough they brushed against her skin as I spoke and she shivered.

"But we can't," she said and her voice was as breathless as I felt.

I continued my exploration until my lips met the shell of her ear. "Wanna bet?"

CHAPTER FOURTEEN

CHARLIE

I COULDN'T SEEM to think straight.

Just like the last time he'd been this close to me, nothing was making sense. I released the death grip I had on his dresser and brought my hands up to his chest, not only to hold him at a distance, but to keep myself upright.

When I didn't answer, he shifted closer. "What were you doing this morning?" he asked, his voice deep and thick with something I'd never heard directed toward me before.

I was lost in it for about two seconds, then I pushed at his shoulders to give me room to breathe—to think. "I don't know what you're talking about," I said, but I couldn't meet his eyes.

His lips came back to my ear with that same voice that made me weak at the knees. "I think I know what you were doing."

"No you don't!" He couldn't. *Oh, God, could he?*

"It's probably the same thing I've been doing in the shower every day since you moved in."

Well, that distracted me from my own mortification. "What?" I shouldn't want to know, but at the same time, now it was all I could think about. This was so bad, but I couldn't seem to pull myself away.

He brought one hand to my mouth where he thumbed my lower lip. I gave up trying to convince myself it was a bad idea and instead focused on drawing in enough air to keep from passing out. His forehead pressed against mine and he exhaled roughly at the same time I drew in a breath. It felt more intimate than any lover I'd had in my short life span, sharing breath with him.

My own eyes shuttered closed and it amplified the sensations of having him so close to me a thousand-fold. The hand at my mouth coasted down my neck, over my collar-bone then down to my trembling hand. He took it in his and that same thumb pressed into the wildly fluttering pulse point at my wrist. Then he palmed my hand and brought it to my waist and turned me around to face the mirror above his dresser.

His lips found my ear again and I met his gaze in the mirror with half-lidded eyes. "I think you were doing this," he said and guided my hand down from my stomach to rest above the waistband of my scrubs.

The drowsy-laziness of arousal snapped clear with recognition, but he wouldn't release my hand when I began to struggle. "I don't know what you're talking about," I said shortly, cheeks burning.

He merely smirked. "I think you know exactly what I'm talking about."

Stubble scraped along my shoulder and I melted a little. "Liam," I warned but I wasn't sure if it was because I wanted him to stop or because I wanted him to keep going.

"Let me show you," he said in that rumbly voice. I had no way to defend myself against it and it was like he knew. Maybe because he knew me better than anyone else in the world. Maybe because I hadn't been able to stop thinkin about him like this. Or the Liam-inspired orgasm I'd had not even an hour before had turned my brain into mush.

That had to be why the words "Show me what?" tumbled from my mouth instead of a refusal.

His hand began to move over mine, this time to guide it further south...and underneath the waistband of my scrubs. "We can't," I said again, but if he stopped I was pretty sure it would kill me. "You have to leave."

"Shh. I'm busy here," he said.

Our hands were over the material of my panties and he was right. There was no point in talking. My throat was so dry I couldn't form any more protestations even if I wanted to.

He nuzzled my ear. "That's my girl."

Seeing us in the mirror and feeling the slow, torturous exploration of our hands together was an assault on my senses, short-circuiting what was left of my self-control. As I gave into him, he guided my hand over my thighs in a gentle, loving caress and for once I was grateful for my scrubs and how easily accessible they were.

With languid strokes, he directed my hand over the tops of my thighs and down between my trembling legs, but never where I wanted him to go. My head dropped back against his shoulder when the sight of us in the mirror became too much for me to handle. He used his free hand to angle my head to the side so he could kiss my neck as he continued the torture.

"I think I've been wanting to do this for a long time. Too long. When I saw you with that jerk and the things he was saying about you. I snapped. It wasn't just because we're friends. It took realizing one day some man is going to propose to you for real for me to wake the fuck up."

My breath caught in my throat as he nudged my hand further between my legs. If I weren't already embarrassed by being caught, the evidence of my arousal dampening my panties would have been enough.

It didn't bother Liam though. As his fingers pushed between mine, he felt the proof for himself. His resulting groan sounded just like the one from my dreams and I fairly collapsed against him in response.

"We should stop," I croaked out even though it was the last thing I wanted.

"No way in hell," he growled.

"But what about—"

He brought my gaze back to his in the mirror. "We don't have to make any decisions now, Charlie. The only thing that matters is that I want you and I think you want me, too. If not, tell me now and I'll stop and I promise you I'll do everything in my power to make sure things go back to normal."

I hesitated, but it was only for a second. If it were anyone else, I would have walked away and not looked back, but it was Liam and it felt righter than anything else in my life. I've spent almost every day feeling uncertain about something. My past, my parents, my future. But I'd never questioned Liam, who'd always been there. I didn't know how this would change everything between us, but I trusted him. Even with my heart.

Even if it scared the life out of me.

"Do you want me to stop?" he asked as he brushed my hand away. He tugged the crotch of my panties to the side and then, with the gentlest touch, pressed the pads of his fingers against me and stole what remained of my resistance.

"Don't stop," I whispered as I wrapped my hand around his neck and pulled his mouth to mine. "Don't ever stop."

"I've got you," he said and despite myself and my fears, I relaxed against him because I believed him.

His fingers parted my folds and I sighed in pleasure. As he rubbed all the sensitive parts of me, it was almost as though he could read exactly what I wanted. Maybe he could. Maybe our years of friendship had prepared him to understand me in ways I'd never anticipated.

"The sounds you're making, Char. God, you're killing me." His lips fluttered against my ear and bucked against him in response.

My fingers latched onto his wrist as my body worked itself to a frenzy. There'd be bruises from the grip I had on him, but I couldn't work up the energy to care. I was so close. Already primed from the orgasm in my bed, it didn't take much from him to bring me back to the brink again.

"Please." My vocabulary had been reduced to one word and I repeated it endlessly. I whispered it. Screamed it. Crooned it. No matter how I said it, he'd murmur sweet words to me in response. He was so patient it made me want to crawl out of my own skin, but he wouldn't let me do that either. Liam merely held me against him as his fingers drove me to insanity.

When I thought he'd never bring me over the edge, he turned my face to his and kissed me. I thought I'd need penetration, at least from his fingers, to finish the job, but no. Everything, it seemed, was different with Liam. All I needed was the sweet, seductive rhythm of his fingers and the gentle pressure of his lips.

The orgasm rolled over me both tender and relentless in equal measure. I whimpered against his lips as it wrecked me from the inside out, leaving me somehow altered in its aftermath. He didn't withdraw his hand at first, merely cupped the delicate flesh until the aftershocks faded.

When the last of the tremors were gone, he turned me in

his arms and tucked me under his chin as his hands stroked over my back and soothed away any doubts I may have had, at least for the moment.

"You okay?" he whispered against my hair.

"That was..." I couldn't find the words because I didn't have any. If I thought there was no going back after the kiss... there was definitely no going back now. What scared me even more than that was that I didn't want to. "That was incredible."

He tipped my chin up and studied my expression. "Are you sure?"

"A little too late to be asking that now."

"Come on, sweetheart. Don't be like that."

I didn't know when shortstack had turned into sweetheart...but I liked it more than I should. It filled my chest with a warm glow—something I'd never had with anyone else. I wasn't sure if it was the orgasm or Liam, or maybe a combination of both, but I *liked* it. It may be a mistake, but I wanted more.

"I'm fine, Liam." I searched his gaze, but found nothing other than concern in his expression. "Are *we* okay?"

The corners of his eyes crinkled and his dimple winked when he smiled. "We're better than okay."

He dove down for another kiss and I promptly decided I could be a few minutes late for work. As we kissed, we stumbled backward until I was bent nearly over the dresser. The edge bit into my back, but I didn't care. I'd had a taste and this time I wasn't going to let anything stop me from getting another.

My phone began to ring in the background, but I'd gotten so many hang ups and calls from random numbers I ignored it. Whoever it was could leave a message.

"You should get that," he said against my lips as his hand molded my breast over my scrub top.

"Later," I replied and fisted his shirt in my hands. "Bed."

He twirled me around immediately and I giggled against his lips. We tumbled onto his bed and he landed on top of me, bracing his arms on either side to catch his fall. My legs parted to make room for him and we both groaned as I pulled him closer.

For the first time in my life, I was considering calling into work to spend the day in bed. I'd never canceled plans for a guy, not even if it was Liam, but as we began to grind together, I was seriously giving thought to changing my mind.

It had never occurred to me before that there would be a guy who could convince me to make an exception.

Or that that guy could be Liam.

Our mouths collided, parted, then collided again. Lips parted, tongues tangled, and teeth clashed until I gave up worrying about work altogether.

My phone began to ring again, but this time it brought back a shock of reality.

We had to stop.

CHAPTER FIFTEEN

CHARLIE

LIAM PAUSED, breathing heavily. "You're right. I have to get to the interview and you have to work."

I nodded even though everything inside me was screaming to keep going. I wanted those clothes off him, wanted to know what it felt like to have his bare skin against mine. More than anything, I wanted to continue what we started, but the annoying blaring from my phone had broken the mood.

"Let me get that," I said, then awkwardly maneuvered to my feet.

"Tell whoever it is to go to hell," Liam shouted at my back as I padded to the kitchen on wobbly legs.

Oh my God, I mouthed to myself when I was out of view. I nearly tripped twice as I made my way to the island to answer my phone.

As I hopped on one foot, I swiped at the screen and

pressed it to my ear. Whoever it was had better be on their deathbed. "Hello?"

"Charlie, thank God. We have an emergency."

Liam walked out and now that I could ogle him without repercussion, my eyes feasted on the way his shirt accentuated the lean muscles of his chest. I'd been this close to having my mouth all over him. *This close.*

"It better be," I said under my breath and Liam smirked.

"What?" Layla asked.

I turned away from him so I wouldn't be tempted to drag him back for another kiss. "Nothing. What's up?"

"My mother is forcing me to attend a mixer tomorrow night with some of her partners from the firm. I need a buffer. Can you come? I promise all the wine you can possibly drink."

I thought of Liam and what we'd come so close to doing... how much I wanted to do it again. "I'm not sure. Where is it?"

She rattled off the name of an exclusive restaurant. "You have to come," she said, sounding desperate, which was out of character for Layla, who valued control above all else. "You can't leave me alone with Dash. His whole family is going to be there apparently and you know how he loves to torment me."

Dash Hampton was Layla's mortal enemy and competitor in all things from parking spaces and lab partners to grades and prestigious honor society positions. They'd been going at it, and not in a good way, ever since he beat her out as Valedictorian their senior year of high school. He and Liam had become friends since Dash liked to hang around specifically to torture Layla at every opportunity. It would nearly be worth going to the mixer just to see the two of them argue. Ember and I used to joke that whenever the two of them were in a room together, it was like getting free entertainment for the evening.

"Why is he even going to be there?" I asked as Liam came up behind me and pressed a kiss to my neck. I nearly dropped my phone as pleasure zinged across my nerve endings. My eyes shuttered closed. He had to stop doing that or we were both going to be late.

"That's what I said," she fairly yelled in my ear, managing to distract me from my Liam-induced stupor. I carefully edged away from him and glared, but he only smiled in return.

"You have to come," she begged. "Otherwise I may commit murder. Save me." I wasn't sure if she realized how often our conversation turned to Dash, but I wasn't about to bring it up. There was no way she was open to a discussion about why she responded to his goading. Hearing his name was enough to make her rant.

"One second," I told her, then muted the call. "If you don't have to work tomorrow with the new job, Layla's forcing me to go to this thing for her mom's firm." I paused, then forced myself to continue. "Do you want to go with me?"

Despite what had just happened between us, my heart

pounded in my chest. I'd never risked so much for anyone before. If it had been any other man, I simply wouldn't have done it. I chose my potential love interests carefully to make sure I wouldn't get overly involved. Apparently, I couldn't seem to follow my own rules when it came to Liam.

He adjusted the cuffs of his shirt and glanced in the mirror above the sofa. "Depending on my shifts if I do, I'd be happy to go with you." When he was satisfied with his appearance, he turned and prowled toward me. "You realize this sounds like a date. You asking me out, Charlie?"

My heart was in my throat. If I had a napkin in my hands it would have been in shreds in seconds. "I know we haven't discussed it, but we hang out all the time. It wouldn't be weird if we went together. We don't have to tell anyone anything. It'd just be hanging out. If you don't want to it's okay, I'd understand."

He smiled and cupped my cheek. "You're rambling. Of course I'll go with you. We don't have to define anything now and we don't have to tell anyone if you don't want to."

I bit my lip. "Are you sure?"

"I'm sure." He kissed my nose, then crossed the room to bend down and pick up his shoes. I guess one of the upsides about living with him now was I could ogle him at every opportunity without being weird.

I had a feeling it was going to become a habit.

After unmuting the call, I said to Layla, "Count Liam and I in."

"YOU SURE you don't mind going with me?" I asked the next day. "I didn't get to talk to you much after you got back from the interview."

I couldn't read his reaction because his arm was thrown over his face. I tried not to notice that his skin was still slightly damp from his workout. The waistband of his sweats rode dangerously low on his hips, leaving my mouth bone-dry.

To say I was *frustrated* was an understatement.

That had to be why I couldn't tear my eyes away from the golden trail of hair dusting his chest and abdomen. It was the only logical explanation for the way my fingers itched to tug down his sweats to see how far down it went. The slight bulge between his legs hadn't escaped my notice, either, but I was trying to be good. We'd kissed twice now. He'd made me come. I wanted to do both again more than I should and I was only one flex of his abs away from begging.

"I already told you I'd go with you, sweetheart. Besides, we have to do something to celebrate my new job," Liam said and I managed, barely, to tear my eyes away from the visual feast that was his body. He caught me staring and grinned. "Unless you'd rather stay home instead."

Heat filled my cheeks and I shifted from foot to foot. "Don't distract me. Layla would kill me if I didn't show up."

He did an ab crunch and his hand shot out to grab my wrist before I could move out of his reach. I squealed as he tugged me down to the bed. "Distract you like this, you mean?"

I should just forget about breathing when he's this close to me, I decided. His teeth nipped at my lips and my mind went blank. "What?"

Liam chuckled and slapped my butt. "You might wanna go get dressed. We don't want to be late for our first official date."

A date. With Liam.

I couldn't seem to wrap my head around it. The little voice that had kept me from getting too into any guy was drowned out by how right it felt being in his arms. Maybe this level of comfort is what I'd be waiting for this whole time. I didn't know how things would change once summer came, but for now...for now I wanted to enjoy him.

"What are you thinking so hard about?" Liam asked as he rubbed the furrow between my eyes.

"Just how crazy this is." I was afraid to even say the words. Maybe that's what had kept me from taking risks in my previous relationships. Why I kept running. I was afraid.

I leapt to my feet and skirted around his bed away from his reach. This could go so wrong. We could come to care for each other and then something could happen and we could break up. These are things I'd hadn't considered until the second he said date. Somehow being around people now made everything real in a way that it hadn't been while we were cocooned in our apartment.

He got to his feet and gripped my biceps. "I've got you, Charlie. I'm not going anywhere."

The knots inside my chest loosened. "I'm being silly."

"You are if you don't get your ass in gear and get dressed. I know you don't want to be late." Using his grip on me, he drew me closer for another kiss.

I practically floated back to my room, heart going a mile a minute as waves of cool air washed over my heated body. Note to self: drink lots of water and wear something breathable. I tore through my closet hoping to find something that straddled the line between indecent and classy because Layla would absolutely flip if I went out dressed in yoga pants again. Focusing on my appearance distracted me from how my lips still tingled from his kiss.

Well, at least a little bit.

I chose a casual but classy dress in siren red that I'd been too shy to wear with anyone else. It would drive Liam crazy and I liked the thought of making him as wild as he made me. I tugged on the dress and imagined how it would feel when he took it off again. A secret smile painted my lips as I ran my hands over the fabric covering my curves.

It's funny, because I used to make fun of the girls who pranced around dressed to the nines or pretended to be obsessed with his interest. They'd flounce around in baseball jerseys because he was a huge Atlanta Braves fan like Tripp or they'd agree to go four-wheeler riding after a hard rain because he enjoyed getting as dirty as possible while going as fast as possible. I never wanted to do those things. In fact, I vehemently protested whenever he'd drag me along to games or kept me out past dark driving through the thick of the woods. I thought I was better than the girls who vied for his attention because I never tried to be the center of it. I got it now. I wanted his eyes on me, no matter what I had to do to get them there. Even if it meant going a little out of my comfort zone.

I zipped up the dress and buttoned the closure at the back of my neck. The keyhole opening at the front showed off just the barest hint of cleavage and the hem of the dress skimmed my thighs. I couldn't keep a tan to save my life, but my legs were toned from hours of being on my feet at work and it had been a long time since I wanted to show them off. I left my hair down and misted it with product to enhance and define the curls. After a quick touch up on my makeup— nothing too dramatic, just a little eyeliner and mascara to define my eyes —I wandered out of my room in search of Liam.

The memories of the girls who used to drool over him had left me feeling vulnerable. We'd explore whatever this was, but I had to remember to be smart while we did. If push came to love, I'd put our friendship first. Always. Relationships came and went, but what we had was timeless.

"Ready to go?" I asked my feet as I pretended to look for something in the small clutch I'd transferred my wallet and keys to.

He didn't answer, but I was hardly paying attention. The

first thing I was going to do when I got to the bar was drink my weight in screwdrivers. Then I was going to find Layla, console her like I always did when her mother decided to focus attention on her. That should give me enough time to figure out how to deal with this Liam thing.

It took me a few minutes of mental preparation to realize he hadn't answered me, so I looked up, my brows drawn and found him staring at me, his eyes stormy and intense. "You okay?" I asked, clutch and personal miseries forgotten. I'd never seen him look at me quite like that before. It made my stomach twist—though not unpleasantly. If I weren't mistaken, he was looking at me the way a man looks at a woman he wanted, badly.

When I managed to tear my eyes away from his expression, I couldn't help but take in the rest of him and, oh, it got better with every. Single. Inch. He wore an old hat he'd had forever pulled down low over his eyes. It cast a shadow over his face, darkening the blonde five-o'clock shadow on his square jaw. He wore a plaid shirt with pearl snap buttons tucked into a new pair of jeans that fit him like a glove. I'd never had an opinion about pearl snap shirts, but they had instantly become my new favorite thing. I couldn't help but think how good he looked, but that he'd look even better if every stitch of it were on the floor.

I swallowed once, hard, and tried to control my breathing. I tried to speak, but my mouth was too dry to form words so I could only stand with my mouth opening and closing like a befuddled fish.

"You look nice," he said and his voice sounded like I felt. My body didn't care about my fears. All it wanted was another tumble on his bed.

"We'd better get going," I said before we did just that.

The dimple in his cheek winked and I knew *he* knew just what I'd been thinking.

CHAPTER SIXTEEN

LIAM

AS A COLLEGE TOWN, Tallahassee, boasted a healthy variety of bars, clubs, and restaurants. A couple years ago, I could be found in any number of them look for a woman, a good time, or both. But I wasn't as interested in the casual thing as I used to be. Swiping through dating apps or trolling the night life for an easy tumble between the sheets wasn't appealing. Probably because it was just that—easy. Not to say I didn't appreciate a woman who knows what she wants, it had just become hollow. The last time I'd taken a woman home, I felt nothing.

I signaled to the bartender for a beer, hoping to feel a little more nothing. I wasn't sure what was worse. The endless line of women, so many at times their faces blurred together, or the thought of risking it all for a woman like Charlie. Just thinking about it made my hands tremble with nerves. The bartender placed a glass in front of me. I took it with one hand and paid with the other, tipping generously for the quick service.

I spotted Charlie across the room and downed half my glass to sooth the rawness in my throat. She'd found her friends Layla--a stunning, if aloof, brunette, and Ember a fiery redhead with a mile-wide smile. They were in the middle of an intense discussion by the looks of it and even though I knew I should look away I couldn't.

She'd pulled her dirty blonde hair over one shoulder and I realized there was a matching cutout on the back of her dress that showed the dip of her spine. I'd never been so irritated and turned on at the same time in my life. I downed the rest of my beer and signaled for another. This one would have to last me the rest of the night because there was no way in hell I was going to let her out of my sight looking as good as she does.

I couldn't take my eyes off her if I tried.

It wasn't the dress, though she looked smoking hot in it, all long legs and shining hair streaming down her back. It was the heated looks she kept sending me and the way her eyes would light up when she caught me looking at her from across the room.

Tripp had come along with Ember and sidled up to me with a fresh beer. I accepted without turning away from the view of Charlie laughing with her friends a little ways down the bar. God, she was stunning when she smiled.

"Hey, man. I didn't know you were gonna be here tonight."

I managed to pull my eyes away from Charlie for a second to find Tripp standing next to me. A starter on the university baseball team, Tripp had been friends with Charlie's friend Ember for as long as I've known them.

"How's it goin'? You here with Ember?"

He signaled to the bartender. "I'll have whatever he's having. Yeah, she didn't want to come alone and begged me to tag along. "Something going on between you two?" he nodded to the three girls across the room.

"What's that?"

Tripp accepted a beer from the bartender. "You and Charlie. Something's different there."

"What the hell is this, social hour? We gossiping now?"

"Spring training. I'm going stir crazy so don't blame me. But you're evading the question, which basically tells me all I need to know."

"What the fuck ever," I said, but we both knew it was just bullshit. I still hadn't taken my eyes off Charlie.

He slapped me on the shoulder, his focus already on a pretty blonde a couple stools down at the bar. I felt for him almost as much as I did for myself. Everyone, and I mean *everyone*, knew he had a huge thing for Ember, but she was dating some grad student who kept stringing her along. Tripp spent most of his time drowning in women to pretend he didn't care about her, even though it was obvious to everyone but Ember.

As he moved in on the blonde, I made my way across the room to the girls. I pulled Layla close to press a kiss to her cheek. "Sorry to interrupt," I told them. "I just wanted to make sure this little lady didn't need a knight in shining armor."

"Thank you, Liam," Layla's eyes were as bright as her smile. "We were just talking about you since you're applying to vet school next semester. Did you get in? I asked Charlie, but she said she wasn't sure."

"Probably the *only* thing she doesn't know about you," Ember said, eyes twinkling. I had a feeling she'd cottoned on to the fact that I hovered close to Charlie's side and had a protective armed around her and propped on the bar.

I could practically feel Charlie vibrating in front of me and it made me want to smile darkly. I'd teased her plenty as friends, but there was a delicious new aspect to teasing her this way. Leaning forward so my lips were just near her ear, I said, "I have a few things to submit for scholarships and I've applied to schools here and a couple other places.

"You have?" Charlie asked twisting around to look at me, her eyes wide.

"Congratulations," Layla exclaimed. "That's amazing. I'm sure you're going to do well wherever you go. I can't believe you haven't said anything!" she added in Charlie's direction.

Charlie just took a sip of her fruity drink, but she'd stiffened against me.

Unable to have her be uncomfortable, I placed a soothing hand around her waist, then said, "I haven't said much about it because I'm still weighing my options. There's been a lot going on, family wise."

"I hear you. The twins are driving me crazy. One of them wants to start ballet, the other one wants to start t-ball. With that, school, and my shifts I can barely see straight let alone apply for scholarships," Ember said, but she smiled. "I don't know how you do it."

Layla and Charlie frowned. "What about your parents?" Layla asked.

Ember gestured to the bartender for another drink and made a noncommittal noise in her throat. "They're both working double shifts. But it's alright. My neighbors watch the kids when I get a call or have to go to class."

"Are your parents still giving you a hard time about going back to school to become a paramedic?" I asked Ember.

She glared at Charlie, who shrugged, which caused her shoulders to brush against my chest. I brushed her hair off her shoulder absently and pressed a kiss to the bare skin there.

Layla and Ember shared wide-eyed looks, but Charlie was too dazed by the casual show of affection to notice. I was glad she wasn't concerned about me kissing her in public. That was progress.

Ember managed answer despite her surprise. "They don't

understand why I want to go back to school when I'm already making decent money."

"You mean they're disappointed you don't devote all of your time to raising their kids?" Layla corrected.

"We're family," Ember replied with a shrug. Her voice cut out and I glanced over my shoulder to see what caught her eye. Tripp and the blonde were in a very passionate lip-lock in a darkened corner. When I glanced back at Ember, a shadow crossed her expression but- it was gone as soon as it appeared. "Besides," she said with faux cheerfulness, "I like Tabby and Nolan. They keep me entertained when Greg is busy and I'm not working."

"You know I'm happy to babysit anytime you need help," Charlie offered.

Charlie's friends weren't my besties or anything, but they were sweet girls who mean a lot to Charlie. So when her offer to Ember made the sweet redhead's sharp green eyes go watery a burst of pride filled my chest. Charlie wasn't just a good friend to me, she was a good person in general.

"Now she's making me look bad," Layla said. "Fine, I'll help you, too. But I do not change any diapers."

We all shared a laugh.

"I think you're safe there," Ember told her. "The twins were potty trained by two."

The two of them had broken the somber mood and managed to distract Ember from Tripp escorting his newest lady out of the restaurant. I doubt Charlie had forgotten about my applying to schools, but she had to know that. Right? My goal was to attend a school here in Florida, if possible, but I'd go wherever afforded me the best opportunity. It was something we'd need to talk about...later. For now, we had a couple hours, an open bar, and some bad food to distract us.

"Layla," came a sharp voice that reminded me all too much of a snake. "Layla Lucille Tate!"

I turned to Layla, who unceremoniously downed the rest of her drink. "You're middle name's Lucille?" I asked with a grin.

She grimaced. "I hate you."

"Don't worry," Charlie rubbed her arm. "We'll be right here."

Layla squared her shoulders and sighed as she crossed the bar area to a woman who must be her infamous mother. She was the spitting image of Layla, only a more severe version. Her dark hair was twisted into a tight bun at the nape of her neck. On Layla the sharp jut of her chin emphasized her fairy-like appearance. On her mother, the sharper edges of her jaw and cheekbones seemed as hard as steel and just as unforgiving.

"What's the story there?" I asked Charlie, who'd turned to lean her back against my arm on the bar.

Ember rolled her eyes and Charlie said, "Layla's mom wants her to go into finance, but Layla refuses. She's wanted to be a teacher her whole life and her mom likes to give her a hard time about it."

I watched as Layla's mom pushed her forward with a claw at the small of Layla's back. A group of fancy suit-types accepted her with fake smiles and her mom beamed proudly. My dad may be overly obsessed with me following in his footsteps, but he'd never treated me like an object or a prize. We didn't get along about everything, but he loved me in his own way. For the first time in a long time, I felt a shred of tenderness for the old bastard.

Maybe I'd give him a call soon.

"I'm gonna go keep an eye on our girl," Ember said as she polished off her own drink, leaving Charlie and I alone.

I twisted around until I had her pinned between me and the bar. "Having a good time?" I asked as I took in the rosiness of her lips and wondered if she'd let me kiss her again. If not here, then when we were back at home, alone.

Suddenly I was very appreciative of my moment of genius. Maybe having her move in with me was the best idea I'd had in a long time.

She licked her lips and nodded. "I am. Thank you for coming with me."

"Should we help Lay and Ember?" The bar wasn't that loud, but I leaned closer like I was having a hard time hearing her. It made me smile when her breath caught in her throat. I enjoyed how much I affected her way too much and wondered if her heart was racing, too.

"What?"

I smiled. "Should we go save Layla from her mom?"

Charlie lifted a hand to my chest and rested it over my heart. Could she tell it was pounding, that she'd brought it back to life? Raised voices from behind me tore me away as I was about to lean down for another taste of her mouth.

A tall good-looking who looked like he'd been born to wear a suit smirked down at a red-faced Layla. Her mother had disappeared, but Layla didn't look pleased with the fact. In fact, if I'd learned anything being raised with sisters, it was how to detect a full-on female rage fest.

"Let me guess," I said as I turned back to her. "That's the infamous Dash?"

Charlie sighed and one side of her mouth curled up. I couldn't tell if she was more amused or resigned. "I should probably go save her. Ember must have distracted her mom."

Before she could slip out of my grasp, I snagged her elbow with my hand. "After you save Layla, do you think we can get out of here?"

Her eyes widened slightly, then heated. She had to clear her throat twice before she could talk. "Yeah, um, just let me take care of this and then we can go."

With my hand on her arm, I pulled her closer. "I think we need to finish what we started yesterday."

CHAPTER SEVENTEEN

CHARLIE

IT DIDN'T TAKE me long to reach Layla's side and tug her away from Dash with a murmured excuse. I don't remember what I said or even if it made sense. All I could think about was Liam's words and getting back to his place. I dropped Layla off with Ember and ignored both of their knowing looks as I sped back to Liam's side. Butterflies were having a rave in my stomach.

"Ready?" he asked as he took my hand and tugged me through the crowd.

I couldn't answer. I let him pull me along until we were back in his truck and heading away from the restaurant. The ride home was a blur. My hands were trapped beneath my thighs because otherwise I'd have them all over Liam's body. Causing a crash would severely wreck my plans for the evening so I kept them to myself.

When he slammed the truck in park with more force than

necessary, I couldn't wait anymore and unbuckled to slither across the seat to his lap.

He hissed out a breath a second before my mouth closed over his. All I could hear was how he was applying to schools everywhere. I knew it in the back of my mind that he'd be leaving, that we both would eventually be busy, but it didn't hit me until tonight. It made me wonder why I had fought so hard to keep from having this with him?

After all, I should know better than anyone that life was short.

His mouth opened under mine and any doubts I may have had washed away as he gripped my hips to keep me close. "I want you," I said against his lips when I could catch a breath. Desperation had me pulling at the collar of his shirt. "Please."

"Jesus, Charlie. Let's get inside before I take you right here."

Somehow we made it out of the truck and to the front door. We slammed against it as I wrapped myself around him. He cursed under his breath as my lips attacked his throat. I moaned as the flavor of him bathed my tongue. It took longer than usual for him to unlock the door because he dropped the keys twice and pushed me against the wall for a kiss that was borderline violent.

We stumbled into the darkened house blind. It was only by pure luck we didn't fall into a heap on the floor. His hands found my hips like they were meant to be there. They slipped around my waist and guided me back down the hall, almost like a dance. My body followed his instinctively, unquestioningly. Somehow, I knew he wouldn't let me fall.

"Are you sure about this?" he asked as we reached the door to his room. "You can walk away right now. Go to your room and get some sleep. You've had a very hard week and aren't thinking clearly. You'll regret this in the morning."

I didn't know if he was warning me, or himself.

It didn't matter, because neither of us listened.

"I can tell you one thing for sure," he said as his lips grew even closer to mine. "The last thing I'd ever regret is being with you."

If I'd had any doubts, his words erased them. I wanted this, I wanted him. "I regret a lot of things, but this would never be one of them."

I didn't want to be alone anymore. I didn't want to keep pushing away the one good thing in my life when life itself was so short. My hands clung to the lapels of his wrinkled suit jacket like he would somehow slip through my fingers. With exquisite care, he peeled my fingers away and pressed them against his chest as he led us back into the shadowed recess of his room. Beneath my hands, his heart thudded in a slow and steady rhythm. I leaned forward and pressed my lips to the triangle of skin bared by the opening of his button-up shirt.

Liam's hands went to grip my biceps, not to push me away or pull me closer, but as a reminder he wasn't quite ready to let me go. Reassured, if only for now, I lifted my fingers to his buttons and fit them through the holes. I bit back a moan of impatience as inch by inch of his tanned throat was revealed.

My fingers dipped beneath the folds of material and I pushed the shirt and suit jacket off his shoulders and down his arms until it fell at his feet. I glanced up at his face to make sure he was still okay and the heat from his gaze made my breath catch in my throat. Determined to keep going, I slid my hands from where they'd stopped at his wrists to the glint of dark blonde hair that lined his abdomen. The moment I touched him, his muscles contracted beneath my hands and he sucked in a breath.

"Don't stop," Liam said through gritted teeth. "Take them off."

As if that was a choice.

Instead of delving into the waistband of his pants like I knew we both wanted me to, I teased us both and slid my hands up his chest and paused at the darker skin of his nipples. My head tilted to the side, and I watched as my thumbs flicked over the sensitive flesh. I glanced up as his face darkened with a flash of need so intense, it was mirrored in my body. My thighs clenched from the emptiness of needing him, but something told me to draw the sweet ache out, make it last.

So I took my time instead. I studied all the parts of his body I'd never given thought to exploring. The dips above his collarbones. The sensitive skin just behind his ears. I covered each discovered spot with kisses and little nips.

He transferred his grip to my hips where his fingers bit into the material of my dress until it stretched skin-tight across my ass. He pulled up my dress until the material gathered at my waist. At the touch of his hands to the tops of my thighs, he groaned in my ear, causing me to shiver. I couldn't seem to get enough of him.

Momentarily distracted, I pressed my face into his throat with my eyes closed to drink in the sensation of having his hands on me. He'd leaned forward to grip just underneath my ass to lift me up. I didn't have time to let out a surprised squeak before we were moving.

He took two quick strides before falling back on the bed with my knees on either side of his hips. Unable to continue my leisurely exploration, my mouth found his with a desperate sound that he didn't hesitate to swallow up. He met my tongue with a thrust of his own and then any attempts at seduction or finesse were lost as I melted against him.

His hands clenched on my ass, causing me to grind into his erection. The old Charlie would have been embarrassed at the brazenness of my actions, but this was Liam, and I couldn't find an ounce of shame inside me for what was happening. There was only the need to get closer, so I didn't hesitate to spread my knees wider and press against him. I couldn't seem to get close enough.

"I can't wait," he said against my lips. "Take off your panties."

Apparently, neither could I.

With jerky, uncoordinated movements, I climbed off him long enough to strip as he grabbed a condom. As I unbuckled his belt and unzipped his pants, Liam tore through my zipper and tugged my dress the rest of the way off and tossed it over my shoulder. My bra and his pants soon followed.

Seconds later, the condom was on and we were reaching for each other. He practically dragged me up his body until I hovered over the hard length of him. Our lips found each other's' and then I lowered myself onto him with a ragged sound. His hand speared into my hair as I began to move over him.

"I can't," I said, but what I meant was, I couldn't wait, but the words wouldn't come out quite right.

"Then don't," he answered.

It was like I couldn't control myself, like my body was saying what I couldn't express in words. I rode him to the brink and came in an explosion that defied logic. I'd wear the bruises from his hands at my hips for days, but reason paled in comparison to wanting Liam as he flipped me onto my back.

I expected him to continue the frantic pace, but nothing could have surprised me more than when he began moving slowly. I tipped my hips up, trying to force him to go faster because my body craved him like nothing I'd ever imagined.

My mind was fevered with need and all I could think about was coming around him again.

"Please," I begged.

Ignoring me, he maneuvered one arm underneath my shoulders so we were pressed against each other from chest to hips. My legs wrapped around his waist and my eyes rolled into the back of my head as he went even deeper. His free hand clutched my thigh as he slid in, then back out with aching slowness.

If my frenzied climb to orgasm had driven all thought from my mind, sending me into outer space, his own chase to the end brought all my thoughts to the forefront, and they all centered around him, around us.

Nothing had ever felt as perfect as being surrounded by him. I wanted to cry at the rightness of it all, but I squeezed my eyes shut and turned into the pillow as he thrust back in, stealing my breath. I'd never known I could be so close to a person. Never known the act of making love wasn't just a physical action.

Whatever was between us wasn't just chemical, it was destiny. Like I'd been searching for the piece to complete me and I'd found it in the last place I'd ever expected.

With my best friend.

"Open your eyes," he said as he canted his hips and made me groan.

I forced myself to look at him, even knowing that when I did it would obliterate me. But denying him was unthinkable.

As soon as I opened my eyes, his hand was in my hair and turning my head up to receive his kiss. My arms wrapped around him, needing to have him as close as physically possible, to anchor him to me when I felt like I was going to simply fly apart.

"Don't leave me," I said in a moment of uncharacteristic transparency. I was so desperate, my nails dug into his back.

"Not goin' anywhere," he said as he shifted to nuzzle into my neck. "I'd never leave you."

Another orgasm threatened causing my breath to quicken. My nails bit a ragged path from his shoulders to the swell of his ass. Even though I was making animal sounds in the back of my throat, he refused to move, which only made me even more frantic. The slickness on his back and the bite rust colored stains on my fingers told me I'd drawn blood in my need to make him move, but he was resolute.

I gave up trying to thrust up to him and instead attacked his mouth with renewed determination. The second our tongues touched, he gripped my hip and shifted his so he wasn't pulling out, but pressing deeper. The sensation of being filled, surrounded, surrendered, overwhelmed me to the point of deliriousness.

I froze underneath him, every muscle inside me going taut as the sweet-hot rush of pleasure overtook me. I'd never felt anything like it, not even close. It was more than just the body-destroying pleasure, more than the physicality of sex. It was the closeness I felt to him that came from our connection.

I clenched around him with a soundless scream that he swallowed. Even though I bucked and rocked underneath him, he was like a mountain being battered by the ocean, and I was the waves crashing against him, reshaping myself to fit around him.

"Open your eyes," I heard through the roaring in my ears.

When I did, he began to move, finally, and I couldn't tell what was better, the way I'd clasped around his stillness or the way each thrust now kicked my orgasm off into new heights.

When he went over, I held him close to me, taking him in as deep as I could and knowing whatever lines we'd unknowingly drawn in the sand between us had just been destroyed completely.

CHAPTER EIGHTEEN

LIAM

CHARLIE WAS the last thing I saw before I slipped into unconsciousness and the first thing I saw when I woke up, and for the barest second I realized that I could get used to waking up to her. I could get used to having her in my bed, her arms wrapped around me and her head resting on my chest. I'd had my fair share of relationships, but no other woman in my bed had ever felt as right as Charlie.

It should have scared the fuck out of me.

I knew when I had time to think with my head instead of my dick that reality would come crashing down eventually. But with her in my arms, all I could think about was having her just one more time. Just one more taste of perfection.

I shifted until she lay on her back and smiled when she made a sound of annoyance. Slowly, as if unwrapping a present, I tugged the sheet down to bare her body and marveled that I'd spent over a decade next to her without taking a bite. She shivered a little from the exposure and her pretty, dark nipples beaded up. Unable to resist, I leaned forward and took one into my mouth to tease it with my tongue. Her hips lifted and her hands slid against the sheets, but she didn't wake.

As I nipped and swirled, I caressed her skin with the back of my hand. Inch by inch, her body woke to my touch. When she was moaning and arching beside me, I moved down the bed to tug off her panties and spread her legs. My mouth watered at the sight of her and I ducked my head to feast.

I started slowly, tracing her wetness with my tongue, searching out the spots that made her come alive beneath my hands. Soon, her fists were gripping my hair and moans erupted from her throat.

"Oh, yes," she said, but her eyes were still closed and her voice soft still with sleep. "Yes."

Her hips bucked against my face, and it was unabashed, unashamed. I couldn't get enough of her response. I wanted her crazy and mindless for me. To wake to the edge of orgasm. To know her first thought was of me, that I'd be as branded on her as she was on me.

Her grip in my hair tightened and her legs by my sides lifted and spread even more. I grabbed the backs of her knees with my hands and pressed them wide and far, pinning them so she was completely vulnerable to me. My tongue engaged in a wicked assault that brought Charlie arching up from the bed, propped up by her hands, her eyes wide and her body on the edge of release.

I paused long enough for a quick, "Good morning," before I was back to driving her crazy.

"Oh, God, Liam. What are you doing?" she said between gasps for breath. "Oh, you have to stop. I can't..."

I gripped her hips more tightly and tilted them up to my waiting mouth. "Yes, you can."

As I watched her resist and then give in, I realized I wanted to do it again and we'd barely even finished. There was something beautiful about seeing her completely exposed and open to me. She'd always been able to tell me anything, but this was different. This was a side of her I never knew existed, and all I wanted to do was figure out what other parts of her I'd been missing.

I couldn't get enough of her taste. I wanted it to coat my tongue. I wanted to drown in her until there was nothing, no one else but her. The thought should have scared me, the intensity should have been overwhelming, but instead it was comforting. Everything inside of me was screaming to take her, to make her mine, but I wanted to give her this first. I wanted to know what she looked like when she went over the edge.

My arms went under her legs and the insides of her calves clutched and gripped at my shoulders, trying and failing to find purchase. Just when I heard her breathing catch, I pulled back and kissed her trembling thighs until her hips bucked up to me, silently urging me to come back to her.

I repeated the languorous teasing until her control broke. Her hands seized on the blankets, ripping them from the bed, searching for an anchor to hold on to. I moved impossibly closer until her hands found my forearms. Even if I had no sensation, I would have recognized the meeting by the deep inhale, by the way the tension melted from her body as our fingers intertwined.

I liked that connection, the way my touch grounded her just as much as my mouth enticed her to fly. My intention was to draw it out, make it last, drive all the doubts out of her mind by pure will alone, but there was something about the taste of her on my tongue that short-circuited my brain.

It started easy. Light teasing nips. The slow pass of my mouth and breath over her sensitive skin. Then languid licks and open-mouthed kisses. She lifted her hips up to meet me and I backed away until she groaned and pleaded. Then the process started all over again. I had myself under control until I followed the taste of her to the source and thrust my tongue inside.

"Liam, oh my God. Omigod." Her desperate words turned into mindlessly whispered pleas, which only served to spur me on.

I used the grip on her hands to pull her whole body closer to me. Without even thinking, she started to lift her hips to meet the thrusts of my tongue. Her hips became unglued and ground against me. I was hard as a rock, but nothing on God's green earth, not even my own discomfort, would have torn me away from the greedy draws of her pussy as she grew closer and closer to the edge of reason.

"Don't stop," I heard Charlie sigh. "Please, don't stop."

Her nails bit into my wrist as I shifted to lift her hips to my mouth. The muscles in her thighs and stomach clenched and her heels dug into my ribs. She was so close, and I'd never wanted anything more than to bring her there.

The strain caused her thighs to shake and I could tell she was holding back. Little growls ripped out of her throat as she chased the edge of release repeatedly. It was only the realization that she was probably thinking too much that tore me away.

She wouldn't look at me as I crawled up her body, but that was okay. I stretched out next to her and pulled her in to my warmth, making sure to tuck the sheets around us. The tension didn't completely go out of her body, but she turned to the circle of my arms, which I took as a good sign. She took in a deep breath and when she let it out, it was a little shaky.

"I'm sorry," she said, and I'd never heard her voice so meek. It made me want to gather her close to me and never let go. Christ.

"Don't be sorry, baby girl. You have nothing to apologize for." I pulled her close to me so she could lay her head on my chest like we'd done a thousand times before. Nothing had ever felt so right.

Only when I thought she was ready, did I place an arm on her thigh. Her heartbeat thundered against my chest, but I merely traced patterns along her skin until it calmed again. Then I increased the pressure of my hands and rubbed all over her stomach and thighs. It was as much to soothe her as it was to keep my hands on her. I couldn't seem to get enough.

With each pass, my hands dipped lower and lower. To the tops of her thighs. The globes of her ass, the small of her back. When I heard her breath catch again, I traced the inside of her thigh with one finger until her legs shifted, allowing me access.

My new favorite thing was listening to her breathing change as my hands mapped her body. I'd never known she could make such erotic sounds and I wanted to catalogue each one. Like how touching the skin just underneath her belly button could make her sigh or how scratching lightly over the backs of her thighs would make her shift and grind closer to me.

I was perfectly content to spend the rest of the morning letting my hands wander over her until there wasn't a part I wasn't familiar with, but she had other ideas. Without warning, she surged up and pulled my mouth down to hers.

"Please," she said against my lips as our tongues battled fiercely. "Please, Liam. Please. Please. Please." She said it over and over until I swore I'd hear her begging in my sleep.

My hands became more insistent, forcing their way between her legs until I found her wet and waiting. I plunged two fingers inside her and swallowed down her moan like it was water and I was two steps away from death.

"Yes," she whispered. "Oh my God, you feel so good. Oh God, please."

She was soaking wet and couldn't keep her hips still, couldn't stop kissing me. Her hands dug into my shoulders and pulled me even closer. I braced myself on one forearm, my muscles burning from the awkward angle, but I didn't dare move. She was clamping down on my fingers and I was so focused on the slow, gliding thrusts that made her plead with me each time I did it that I didn't care if I had to hold this position for the rest of my life.

When she went over, God, I didn't think I'd ever forget how she felt in my arms. She tugged me closer to kiss me wildly, open-mouthed and animalistic. She rode my fingers until her hips couldn't move any longer and I pulled back just enough to commit her pleasure-ravaged face to memory.

CHAPTER NINETEEN

CHARLIE

I SHOULD HAVE BEEN EMBARRASSED, but somehow, there wasn't room for it. I'd never been so comfortable with another man before. It didn't make any sense to me because it should have been awkward. I'd known Liam so long in every other way, him seeing me naked, him making me come should have made me want to run in the other direction. But it didn't.

It made me want to climb on top of him and do it again.

All I wanted to do was sink against him and stay in the protective circle of his arms. I'd always been relaxed around him, but this was different. It was as though I'd discovered another side of him, one that fit all my jagged edges like the perfect matching puzzle piece.

I blinked up at him, my tongue thick and heavy in my mouth. I didn't know what to say, but he seemed to know what I wanted without words and simply put a hand on my waist and wrapped me up in his arms, just like I needed.

I'm not normally a crier, but my chest swelled with emotions I didn't know how to handle. Instead of letting them out, I balled my free fist up in the sheets to cover his stomach and pressed my forehead against his chest. The hand on my back rubbed over me in a soothing gesture until my breathing went back to normal and all the blood returned to my brain.

"Wow," I said, when I could think again. "Just...wow."

He chuckled and pressed an absent-minded kiss to the top of my head that made it hard for me to swallow. "Good morning?"

"Very," I answered. I exhaled shakily. "Very good morning."

"You okay?" he asked, his mouth still resting against my hair.

"I think so."

He started to speak, but my phone cut him off. "Hold that thought. Some rando's been calling me for weeks. Let me tell them to stop calling," I said as I reached for it. "Hello?" But it came out split into two words because the second I answered, Liam's hand streaked up my thigh. I held it with one of my own.

"Hello?" came the tentative answer. "Is this Charlie St. James?"

The hand climbed higher, despite my grip on it. "S-speaking." I glared at Liam, but there wasn't a shred of regret to be found. As soon as the call was over, I was going to tease him until he begged for it.

"You sound just like me. I can't believe it's really you."

My hand went limp on Liam's and my heart began to race. "Who is this?" I scrambled for an explanation, but my mind was blank.

"Do you have a minute to talk?" came the woman's answer. I didn't recognize her voice. She said I sounded just like her, but I didn't note the resemblance. Besides, why would I sound like her? That didn't make any sense...

Then it hit me. I sat up straight, racing heart now in my throat. "Who is this?" I repeated. My voice was harsh, almost a bark, but I didn't care. "Tell me or I'm hanging up."

"Don't hang up. Please. I just want a chance to explain."

"Start talking, then."

Liam sat up against the headboard and his arm came around me until his hand rested reassuringly on my thigh. "What's the matter?" he murmured.

I could barely hear him or the woman on the phone over the ringing in my ears.

"This is April. April Parrish." She laughed nervously. "I'm, God, I'm your mom, Charlie."

"P-Parrish. April Parrish," I repeated to make sure I was hearing things correctly. The word "Mom" ricocheted in my skull. I'd played this scenario over and over again in my head, but I never truly believed I'd ever hear from her again. Now that I had her on the phone, I didn't know what I wanted to say first, if anything.

"Yes, baby, it's me. God, it's been such a long time."

"Mom?" Someone answered. It took me a minute to realize the small sounding voice was my own.

"Mom?" Liam repeated. His hand tightened on my hip. I covered it with my own and squeezed, needing the reassurance his strength provided.

"I know. I can't believe it either," she said. I had to close my eyes to focus on the sound of her voice. She was right. I could recognize my own in hers. "I was at work and I came across your application for the volunteer trip. I almost couldn't believe what I was reading. It took me weeks to work up the courage to call you."

"You work for the volunteer organization?"

"Sort of. It's hard to explain, but I'd love to meet you in person. If you're up to that, I mean. I want to help you."

"Help me?"

"With the application. I know some people and thought I might push it along so they see it? If you were interested, I mean."

The happiness I'd felt waking up to Liam had leached away the moment I answered the phone and realized who was on the other line. "Why would you want to help me now?" I asked.

Liam's hand tightened on mine. I squeezed back for dear life, a little more at ease knowing that no matter what happened, he was there for me.

"I know nothing I say can ever explain away what I've done, but I thought, maybe it was a sign. Maybe I enough time has passed that we can maybe talk again. Nothing I say will ever explain away what I did, but I'd like the chance to give you my side of the story."

"Why should I?" I asked bluntly.

There was a pause before she said. "I thought you might like the chance to get to know your family."

"My family?" My throat closed around the words.

"Please, Charlie. Just give me a chance."

I hung up a few minutes later and slumped against the headboard, unsure of what to think. My mom. I'd just talked to my *mom*. I wanted to cry. I wanted to scream. I wanted a million different things and didn't know which one of them I should do first.

"Are you okay?" Liam asked quietly.

I shoved my face in my hands and sucked in a deep breath, but it didn't help. "I honestly don't know."

He kissed my shoulder and his breath fanned over my still-bare skin. I'd forgotten I was naked, but as soon as I realized it and how close he was, my body heated. Despite the shock, it still wanted him. I wanted him.

"Is there anything I can do to help?"

I turned to lean my head against his chest and my muscles relaxed as his warmth seeped into my clammy skin. "Just stay with me for a while, please."

"Of course." His hands traced my body, causing me to shiver. "Do you want to talk about it?"

I shrugged. What was there to say? I still couldn't believe what had happened. "She wants to meet me. To talk."

"Are you gonna do it?"

I closed my eyes and fitted my face into his neck. As though we'd done it a thousand times, he shifted to make room for my body. "I'm not sure."

"Whatever you decide, I'm sure it'll be the right thing." How he could be so certain, I'd never know. What I did know was he was my rock. The solidness of him beside me quelled the panic that threatened to rise.

Silence surrounded us, but it wasn't uncomfortable. Then I tilted my head back to look at him. "Will you do me a favor?"

He brushed the hair away from my face. "Anything," he said.

"Will you help me forget, just for a little while?"

His hand trailed down my arm, pushed beneath the sheet covering my bare hip and cupped my ass. "You mean like this?"

"Yes," I said on an exhale. "Please."

His voice dropped an octave. "I love it when you say that."

I strained upward until my lips reached his ear. "Please, Liam."

He groaned and settled between my legs. "Whatever you want, sweetheart. I'll give you whatever you want."

He slid inside, and I gripped his arms. "All I want is you."

AN HOUR LATER, we were running very late to meet up with the girls, Dash, and Tripp for dinner and drinks. Since we all lived in the same building, we normally met at Ember's place on the first floor since it was the most convenient. She'd offered to let me stay with her, but her twin brother and sister slept over her place as often as they did her parents. Ember had enough on her plate and I didn't want to be a burden.

"Sorry we're late," I said as I stumbled into her living room, tugging on my cardigan sleeve and trying not to blush. Liam had done exactly as I asked and made me forget everything but him. "I was doing...stuff."

Liam emerged from the door behind me with a self-satisfied smile on his lips. "I was stuff."

I slapped him on the shoulder, then shoved him into the wall. I turned, sniffed, then said, "Did someone save me a slice of ham and pineapple?"

Ember and Layla shouted, "I knew it!" at the same time and Dash and Tripp shared manly grins with Liam.

It wouldn't make our problems go away and we'd have a lot to talk about eventually, but for now, I had my friends and

I had Liam and that was all I needed to forget everything else and lose myself in the moment for once instead of worrying.

CHAPTER TWENTY

LIAM

I LEFT Charlie in my bed the next day without waking her.

Not only because she looked so peaceful as she slept, but because I knew if I looked into her eyes I wouldn't be able to do what I needed to do without feeling overwhelming guilt. But it didn't matter. I still felt regret gnawing away at my insides like a cancerous tumor. I rationalized it by telling myself there was no use in bringing up the scholarship as my options were still wide open. The last thing she needed right now was for me to bring up that I was applying to veterinary schools out of state.

The ride to the library on campus took for-fucking-ever and gave me too much time to think. Too much time to remember how Charlie looked the moment she took me inside her. How she made me feel like I was the only man in the world, in her eyes. It was heart-stopping, the way she looked at me.

I used to think I knew everything about her. I could tell by the sound of her voice if she was happy or sad. I could read her like a fuckin' book.

But the past couple days.

They'd been different.

They'd been more.

And it scared the fucking shit out of me.

It made me want things I shouldn't want.

Things I don't deserve.

She makes me want it all—with her.

I had to force all of it—including her—from my mind as I reached the parking garage for the library. The scholarship was for the University of California, Davis. It had been my first choice after the University of Florida. Or at least it had been before I realized how far away I'd be if I got it. How far away I'd be from Charlie.

I used to think being with Charlie was a simple as breathing. Now I realized it was so much more than that. Being around her was as essential, as life-giving, as necessary. The thought of losing her sent my body into an all-out panic. My chest ached and my brain screamed for just one more inhale.

I knew reality would return when deadlines for admission came, along with all my doubts, but for that moment, I wanted to breathe her in over and over, until she's was as much a part of me as the oxygen flowing through my veins. I wanted to enjoy having her by my side for as long as I fucking could.

Each step I took through the cavernous lobby put more and more distance between me and the one person I never thought I could abandon. I could feel myself moving father and father away from her, but I knew we'd both regret it if I put my plans on hold. Despite everything that had happened, we both had a future.

As I sat at the desk to review my paperwork, I realized I'd never considered the fact that our futures might not be with one another. And that thought scared me more than it should.

I was so troubled by the thought I pushed it from my mind and called my dad to stop from thinkin about it.

"Hello," he answered after a couple rings. I had to press my ear close to the speaker because my dad had a habit of getting distracted and not speaking directly into the microphone.

"Hey, Dad, it's Liam."

"Liam. Good to hear from you."

I cleared my throat. "You too. Uh, listen, I'm being considered for a couple scholarships for veterinary school and I need your help with the financial information. They're requesting copies of tax returns for the past couple years for verification."

Dad grunted.

"Would you mind emailing me copies, please? I don't have them and they need them in the next couple weeks before they announce finalists."

I didn't try to explain to him what the scholarships could

mean for me. They were the difference between attending a top school in the country or settling for my second choice. The truth was, I wasn't sure he'd care about the difference. As far as he was concerned, I was chasing a pipe dream.

"Yeah, I'll see what I can do."

"It's that William?" came Grandma Dorothy's voice.

"It's Liam, Mom," Dad corrected solemnly.

I felt like a dick. Dad was just trying to do what was best for his family. He probably couldn't understand why I wanted to become a vet despite that I'd tried to explain it to him several times. He had to put his mother in a home rather than take care of her. Much as we butted heads, I needed to remind myself to cut him a break.

"Liam!" came Grandma's familiar voice as she took the phone. "I miss you baby boy. When are you going to come see me again?"

I thought of upcoming exams, work, and the acceptances I needed to sort through and make a decision about. "I'm going to try to head over there as soon as I can, okay?" I hated telling her no, but there was so much I needed to do.

"Oh, alright. Well, I miss you and I love you!"

"I love you to, grandma. Give mom a hug for me."

"I will, baby. You take care of yourself."

"You, too," I answered, but she was already gone.

~

AFTER A LONG DAY of classes and worrying about grandma, I was looking forward to going home, and if I was honest, seeing Charlie. We'd texted throughout the day, but I wanted to bury myself in her and forget everything else. I'd spent an hour at the gym after my last class, but it still didn't erase the unease pulling at my stomach. The only thing in my life that seemed to be going right was her...and I didn't want to lose her.

The scent of spices and grilling meat greeted me the second I opened the door and nearly brought me to my knees. I immediately made a mental note to give her the hardest orgasm of her life. It was like she knew I needed to come home to something like this today. I don't know how she knew, but I was grateful.

"Something smells good," I said as I dropped my stuff by the door and crossed the open living room to where she stood by the oven smiling at me.

"I hope you don't mind. After work I was craving some red meat."

I wrapped my arms around her waist as she stirred what looked like mashed potatoes in a pot. My mouth watered, but it wasn't only for the food. "Mind? I think you're an angel."

"You better quit it," she said when I started nibbling on her ear. "If you don't I might burn the food."

I backed away to sit at the island, but my eyes were on her. "Fine, but only because I'm starving. First I'll eat dinner, then I'll have you for dessert."

Her cheeks grew rosy and I smiled, feeling the tension leaving my body. "Is it always like this?" she asked as she turned back to add butter, salt, and pepper to the mashed potatoes.

I take a sip from the beer she'd already had waiting on the counter while I considered my answer. "What do you mean?"

She didn't turn to face me as she spoke. "I've never felt like this about anyone before. I never let myself. But I already care so much about you, it's like there's no stopping it now."

The beer washed away the knot in my throat. "Come here," I told her and she did as I asked. I pulled her between my legs so I could look into her eyes. I could have told her it was normal, that every relationship feels as intense as the connection between us, but I couldn't. "No, it isn't always like this."

"Is it because we're friends?"

Sitting down she was the perfect height for me to pull her lips to mine. "I don't have an answer for that," I said against her mouth. "But what I do know is I care about you. A lot. More than I have for any other woman. I didn't plan for this to happen, but I'm glad it did."

She let me take the kiss deeper until the kitchen timer trilled. "I better get that," she said and I was pleased to find she was little out of breath. "I have something to ask and if it's too much you can say no."

"What is it?"

"Will you go with me to meet my mom tomorrow?"

CHAPTER TWENTY-ONE

CHARLIE

"YOU'LL STAY WITH ME?" I hated that my voice wavered. I didn't want to care that I was about to see my mother for the first time in over half my life.

Liam squeezed my hand, reminding me that I wasn't alone. "Of course I will. I'm not going anywhere."

From my vantage point in a booth at Chinese restaurant I'd chosen, I noted parking lot was as empty as it had been for the past ten minutes. Part of me was afraid she wouldn't show. I almost hoped she didn't. It would be so easy to spend the rest of my life blaming her for everything that had gone wrong. Or maybe she would show and be worse than the villain I'd conjured in my mind. Someone I could pity and forget.

Normally, I loved the scents that wafted from the kitchen. Warm sesame oil, searing meat and garlic. Now they only exacerbated the nausea. A warm hand caressed my hip and settled on my waistline. Liam tugged me to his side and I closed my eyes against the vision of the parking lot and the images of my mother, pressing my face into the curve of his neck. He tucked his hand between my thighs and kissed my hair. As I snuggled closer in the booth facing the plate glass of the front window, I wondered how we'd spent so much time together without ever knowing how good it would feel to be this close.

"Thank you," I said.

"For what?" he asked.

"You know what."

I peered through my lashes, unable to keep them closed for long, but didn't see anyone I recognized outside the restaurant. Would I even recognize her? Would she look like me? I had pictures from when I was little. There weren't many because I think Dad got rid of a lot of them, but I couldn't tell from the ones I had.

Liam squeezed my hand. "You don't ever have to thank me for being here for you."

"Still," I said, squeezing back.

The parking lot was empty except for Liam's truck, so I knew the moment a small red Corolla pulled in that it had to be her. My whole body stiffened and Liam sat up to rub his hand over my arms to soothe me. Normally it would work and I'd melt into him, but no amount of touching could get me to settle right now.

Oh, God, this had been a bad idea.

I never should have agreed to meet her. What answers was she going to give me that I didn't already have? She wouldn't bring my dad back. She couldn't give me the family I'd been without. Liam's family had taken that place. His parents, sisters. Grandma Dorothy. Him.

But I had to at least give her a chance. That's why, as she pushed into the restaurant and peered around, I didn't duck into the bathroom to hide from her like the coward I was. When her eyes locked on me, I felt her gaze like a shock. She even had my eyes. The same dark green eyes stared back at me for a long moment before her mouth curved in a tentative smile.

Liam's phone rang and he sent me an apologetic look and went to silence it. "No," I told him as I laid a hand on his arm. "It's okay. I'm okay. Why don't you take the call while I talk to her?"

He hesitated, the phone still ringing in his hand. "Are you sure?"

I nodded as she reached the table. "I'm sure. Just stay close in case I need you."

"I'll be just outside." He inclined his head toward my mother in greeting before answering the call and stepping outside.

"Charlotte?" she asked, and I only barely kept from wincing.

"Charlie," I corrected.

Chagrined, she set her purse down on the table in front of

her and knotted her hands. "Right, sorry. Charlie. Wow, you look just like your father," she blurted.

I touched my hair self-consciously. It was the same golden-blond his had been. "Really?" The off-handed comment meant more to me than she could possibly know.

"It's uncanny." I didn't know her well enough to guess, her voice thickened at the mention of him. "I was sorry to hear when he passed. Even more sorry when I never called to explain and when I didn't come back."

My mouth was so dry my tongue was glued to the roof of it. "Why didn't you?" I asked when I managed to unstick it. Apparently, it had freed the very question I had buried deep down inside of me. I hadn't wanted to ask that the first time I saw her, hadn't wanted to let myself be vulnerable, but it was out there and I was completely bare to this person who had abandoned me when I needed her the most.

She looked to her knotted hands as she spoke. "I wish I had a better answer for you, Charlie, but the truth of the matter is I was very young when your father and I got married. Very young, and very unprepared. When you came along, I thought it could fix the broken relationship between us, but it didn't."

"So you think that's a good reason to abandon him?" My voice was sharper than I intended. Anger burned low in my belly. I'd coached myself not to get too emotional when I finally saw her again, but no amount of preparation could stop the words from spewing forward.

She shook her head and looked down at her hands. She'd taken a napkin from the dispenser and had begun tearing it to shreds in front of her. That more than seeing her again, more than speaking to her speared me right in the gut. How else were we alike?

"I didn't want to leave, but nothing we did seemed to work. The more I tried, the more he turned to caring for you. Not that it was your fault. You were the best thing that ever happened to us, but when he got sick I couldn't face losing him. It was too much."

"Too much for you?" I scoffed and resisted the urge to get my own napkin to rip to shreds. God knew I wanted to rip something. "What about me? I was just a teenager. You left, and then he died, and I was all alone."

"There are no explanations for the things I've done. No apologies. I know I don't deserve a chance at getting to know you, I certainly don't deserve to be forgiven."

"Then what do you want?" I demanded.

"To give you something back for what I've taken away. Let me help you with this volunteer thing. Please, you don't have to do anything for me. I don't know any other way to say I'm sorry."

"I'm not saying I will, but first you have to answer a question for me. Why didn't you come back when he died? When he left me all alone with no one?" My voice was higher than I'd intended, and I lowered it a few octaves. "Why didn't you come back for me then?"

She couldn't look me in the eye. "I was ashamed and I felt like your life would be better, less complicated and happier if I weren't in it."

I was silent for a few moments while I digested the news. "Then why did you reach out to me now? What's different?"

Her eyes brightened and one of her hands went to her stomach. "I met someone. Someone who truly cares for me. I've changed a lot in the past few years and I wanted to give you—us—the opportunity to have a relationship, if you wanted. The man I married is a good man. He wanted our daughter to know you, too."

"I have a sister?"

She smiled the first real smile since she walked in the door. "You do. You have a whole family now, Charlie. And I'd like you to meet them."

WE WERE silent on the drive back to the apartment. I'd spoken with my mother for another hour with Liam by my side after our initial conversation. She told me she had steady work as a volunteer with the organization planning my trip abroad and about her husband—my stepfather—John. She invited me to their anniversary barbecue the following week-end. I wasn't sure if I was going to accept, or if I'd even see her again, but I felt better knowing instead of guessing about who she was and where she'd gone.

Liam took my hand as we walked made our way to the front door. So much had changed in such a short time since I'd moved in with him. His parents selling the farm. We were both having to make decisions about our careers soon. My mother. God, I had a whole family out there I'd never known about and I didn't know how to feel about it.

"Do you want to talk about it?" he asked when we got inside.

I shook my head. "I will, eventually, but right now, I just want to be with you for a while. Everything else may not make sense, but when I'm with you, when you touch me, it's like I'm right where I'm supposed to be. Is that okay?"

"That's more than okay," he told me as he wrapped his arms around me. "I'm here for whatever you need."

I tugged him down with me to the couch, needing the security of the weight of him pressing me into the fabric. Nothing felt as good as having him surrounding me. I'd never felt more at home than I did in his arms.

Only a few days ago this space had seemed so small with the two of us in it. I'd wanted to run, needed room to breathe. Now, with Liam, it had become my refuge, my sanctuary. Hell, it could have been as tiny as his room and I would be perfectly content to spend the rest of my life in less than 1000 square feet.

When I kissed him, it was full of desperation. I ripped off his shirt, needing to feel his skin to ground me, to steady me. Even if everything else in my life was uncertain, the one thing

I could be sure of was this, him. And for now that was enough.

If our first time having sex had been an adventure and our second a free-fall, the feeling that overtook me as I clung to Liam was desperation. There was an edge to my need that even I couldn't understand. An edge that made me cling to his arms a little tighter, lean in to him a little closer, savor his kiss a little more.

An edge that made me realize once more that some good things just don't last forever. And I should cherish them—him —while I was able.

CHAPTER TWENTY-TWO

LIAM

"ARE you sure you don't want me to stay home with you today?" Charlie leaned a shoulder against the door jamb and studied me as I got dressed.

"Not gonna say it again, Charlie. I'm fine. I don't need you to hover." If my tone was a little short, I hoped she'd forgive me. I'd make it up to her later.

"I'm not hovering. I can tell you're upset about Grandma Dorothy. I am, too, but she needs to be somewhere with constant care."

I hated that I wasn't going to be at home to be there when Grandma was transferred to elder care. I hated that my father had rubbed it in my face the last time I called to check in on the forms I needed. "I know that."

She crossed the room and stopped me from putting on my hoodie as I prepared for a run. "You should go see her this weekend."

"I can't I have to work. You know that." My new job didn't have substitutes and I was under a probationary period. Calling into work wouldn't endear me to my new boss who had been hesitant to hire me considering I'd been let go from the last place.

She frowned. "I was so excited for that new job, but it's keeping you busy."

"Gotta pay rent somehow." I didn't say it, but I also needed the money to save up to move...if and when I chose a school for next year. I was already cutting it way too close for comfort, but I needed those papers from my father, who hadn't returned my messages about the forms I needed.

"Do you want me to go with you?" she asked.

"Please. You hate running."

She laughed and it lightened my worries, if only a little. "That's true."

I kissed her lightly on the lips. "Don't worry about me, sweetheart. I'll be fine. Besides, don't you have a final to be studying for?"

She pouted. "It's not fair you already finished yours."

Deepening the kiss helped to distract us both. "Why don't you finish up studying while I'm gone and then we'll have something to eat. I'll cook this time," I added before she could offer. "You've catered to me more than enough."

Tossing her hair over her shoulder, she smirked at me. "Is that what you think?" she asked.

I noted the look in her eyes and carefully put distance

between us. "Oh, no you don't. You're not going to distract me when you have to study. You know we won't get anything done if we get back in bed."

It was the truth. Now that we'd crossed that line, we couldn't seem to get enough of each other. I'd thought the need for her would have cooled eventually, but if anything it seemed to burn hotter each time I had her.

She gave me that look that meant she wanted me, now. It was a look she knew I couldn't resist. "Charlie," I groaned. "We can't do this now."

"Hush," she said and covered my lips with her fingers. "Let me do this for you."

"You don't have to *do* anything for me."

"I want to."

She dropped her hand and then fell to her knees in front of me. There wasn't time for me to prepare because a second later, she pulled down my cotton running shorts and had me in her mouth.

"Jesus fucking Christ," I said as the wet heat of her mouth enveloped me. She took me deep, stroking my dick with her tongue as she sucked me.

I scooped up her hair with both hands and tried to slow her down, but she wasn't having any of it. She gripped the base of my dick and stroked with each slide of her mouth. My legs shook and I gave serious consideration to collapsing back on the bed. She devastated me.

I wish I could say I lasted a long time. I wish I could say it didn't completely wreck me when she glanced up at me, but I couldn't. It only took a few minutes for me to reach the point where I tried to pull her away. We'd never really talked about things like *swallowing* for fuck's sake, but she wouldn't have any of it. She sucked me back even farther and stroked harder with the tight fist of her hand.

"Charlie," I groaned. "You gotta stop."

But she didn't.

I hunched over as the orgasm hit and I came into the sweet recesses of her mouth. She didn't stop for a second. Watching her throat work as she swallowed it down had to be one of, if not *the*, hottest moment of my life.

She rocked back on her heels after licking me clean and I pulled my shorts back up. It had only been a few minutes, but I felt like I'd run a marathon.

"Now you can go," she said with a laugh as she got to her feet with a wicked smile.

I stood there for a minute hoping my legs would hold me up. "I'm not sure I can."

Charlie began to back away. "You go for that run. I'm going to study. You definitely owe me dinner when you get back."

Somehow I made it to the front door without falling straight on my face. I shook my head as I stretched on the front porch. That girl was something else. Despite the growing realization Grandma Dorothy was never going to get better and everything else going on in my life, Charlie was the bright post. She always had been. I couldn't imagine my life without her.

God, I loved her.

The thought stopped me short as I reached the trail around Lake Ella opposite my house.

I loved her.

What the hell was I going to do about that?

CHAPTER TWENTY-THREE

CHARLIE

I WOKE up to a snoring Liam and I immediately smiled.

I was doing a lot of smiling around him lately. It was like I couldn't contain it. I was stressed about my mom, stressed about finals, and the final approval for volunteering, but as soon as I walked in the door it was like his mere presence could wash it away.

As I shifted, he cracked open an eye and smiled. His arms wrapped around me and he pulled me closer to kiss my hair. "Good morning, beautiful," he said, like he had every morning after I slept in his bed.

"What?" he asked when I didn't respond right away.

I pressed my forehead against his chest which, was warm from our combined heat under the sheets. Our skin stuck together where arms and legs were intertwined. I was completely wrapped up in him, under his spell. I nuzzled into the thin dusting of hair on his chest and suck in heady breaths heavy with the scent of him. The last wispy remains of yesterday's cologne and the cotton fresh laundry detergent he prefers.

"I like waking up to you," I told him with uncharacteristic honesty. It was akin to me offering him my heart on a silver platter. I wanted him to see me bare and defenseless, with walls down. For the first time, I wanted to let a man in, rather than barricade him out.

His hand brushed over my hair and I stretched like a cat against him. "Oh, do you?"

"I like the way you hold me."

His arms tightened around me. "Good luck trying to get me to let you go."

If I'd thought he couldn't get any more amazing, I was wrong. And that was after an amazing night with him once he got back from his run.

It hadn't been anything special, but to me, it was everything. We ate dinner and watched a movie cuddled together on the couch. I studied to the point where I couldn't see straight and he forced me to take a break, which of course meant we ended up making out on the couch until three o'clock in the morning.

I swear, I wish we'd made the plunge into dating sooner. I've never felt about anyone the way I feel about him.

It was as simple as feeling his heart beat sync with my own. He twined his fingers with mine and pressed them against his chest.

The words spilled out before I even made the conscious thought to say them. "I love you, Liam."

His body stilled under my hands and with anyone else, I would have rushed to apologize. To backtrack and take apologize. At the first sign of commitment or weakness, my first instinct was normally to run, but the only running I wanted to do when it came to Liam was right back into his arms.

When he didn't say anything, the first tingling of anxiety had me tilting my head back to gauge his reaction. I found him smiling down at me and taking my lips for a kiss I'd never forget.

"I love you, too, Charlie," he said when we stopped to catch our breath.

I dragged him back to me as warmth spread through my chest. My whole body felt as though it were weightless. I couldn't stop smiling even though we were kissing. By the time we were done, happy tears had blurred my vision.

"I hate to tell you this," Liam said as he looked over my head. "But I think you might be late for that final."

Still floating from the kiss, it took me a minute for the meaning of his words to sink in. "What?" I shrieked and flew from the bed. "Oh my god, I'm so screwed."

I stumbled across the hall to my room and grabbed at clothes blindly. I'm not sure any of it matched, but I didn't care. Failing this final would ruin me for the whole semester. Liam was waiting for me in the kitchen with a steam carafe of coffee. If I hadn't already fallen in love with him, seeing him standing in his boxers with just a mug of coffee would have done it.

"You're a god," I told him as I accepted the carafe and gave him a quick kiss. "See you later?" I threw over my shoulder as I hurried to the door.

"I'll be here," he replied.

On my way to campus I sped through more yellow lights than I cared to admit. Speed bumps? More like suggestions. I only had two minutes to get to the final before the professor, who was notorious for locking doors on the hour, barred me from entering. I was just pulling into a spot when my phone rang.

Thinking it could be Liam, maybe hoping it would be, I answered. I was turning into a fourteen-year-old with a crush. I was smiling when I said, "Hello?"

"Charlie, I'm glad I caught you." I recognized April's voice. I wasn't quite ready to settle on calling her mom again. I might not ever be.

"April? I'm running kind of late for an exam can I call you back?" My lungs burned with effort as I raced from student parking to the building where the final was taking place.

"This will only take a second," she said.

"Good, because that's all I've got."

"I received word that your application has been accepted. The volunteer spot is yours if you want it."

The news should have made me happy, but if it did, it was hollow. I frowned as I shoved through the double doors and hurried down the hall. "That's great," I told her. This was all I'd wanted for a long time. The chance to serve where I was needed, to give back to others the way I wanted to when my father was sick, but couldn't. It's the entire reason why I decided to get my bachelor's in nursing in the first place.

There was a pause. "You don't sound as enthusiastic as I thought you would."

I tried to muster some enthusiasm up. "No, I am, this is great."

She cleared her throat. "Look, I don't mean to be rude, but I pushed your application through. I had to pull some strings to get you accepted. I thought you'd be pleased."

My back stiffened. I wanted to close the gap between us, but I certainly didn't need her playing mother. "You shouldn't have done that. I didn't need your help. I would have gotten it on my own."

"I just wanted to help you."

I took the stairs two at a time and cursed under my breath. One minute. "Look, I'm grateful for your help, but my plans may have changed."

"Changed?" There was a pause. "This is about that boy isn't it. The one who was at the restaurant with you? Please don't tell me you're throwing this opportunity away for some guy."

I thought I'd gotten over her leaving. In fact, I was looking forward to meeting her family and mending fences. The second she attacked Liam however, I snapped. "Funny coming from a woman who threw away her daughter." I reached the classroom door just as the professor was walking up the aisle to lock it. "I've got a final, I have to go."

Click.

Pushing her from my mind, I gave my professor a nervous smile and took a seat in the back of the room. She had no right to judge any choices I made. Just because I was no longer obsessed with school and my career, didn't mean they still weren't important.

I was allowed to have a life in addition to work. In fact, I'd given it up in exchange for extra classes, volunteer work and my job for so long I'd forgotten what fun was like until recently. She had no right to tell me what to do, especially after she'd been absent for so long.

If I wanted to give up the volunteer opportunity to spend more time with Liam, there'd be other chances.

I couldn't say the same for me and Liam. We only had a couple short weeks before his lease ended and we had to make a real decision about what was happening between us.

For the first time in my life, I was open to the possibility of taking a chance.

As long as it was with him.

CHAPTER TWENTY FOUR

LIAM

MY EMAIL DINGED as I was driving home from work later that day and I paused at a stoplight to check it. *Dear Mr. Walsh, unfortunately you are ineligible to receive the scholarship based on...*

A loud blare from the car behind me shook me out of my stupor. I ground my teeth together as I accelerated. I'd been so distracted the night before I'd forgotten to call and remind dad to submit the forms so I could finish the application by the deadline. The email had been a standard form rejection. With only a few words, my hopes at attending the best school in the country had been squashed.

Part of me had to wonder if it hadn't been a deliberate move on Dad's part. Now he had me right where he wanted me. I'd attend the University of Florida, which was a couple hours away but still close enough to stay under their thumb. I should be grateful I was accepted anywhere, that a partial scholarship I'd already received would cover some of the costs, but all I could think about was the opportunity I'd lost.

Because of him.

Charlie's car was already parked next to my space. I needed to talk to her about what was going to happen this summer, but I didn't know what to say. How do I tell her I have to leave her when just this morning I'd told her I loved her?

Dread pooling in my stomach, but I strode to the front door in spite of it. I'd just tell her. She'd understand. Charlie always understood. We'd just have to make it work somehow. People did that sort of thing all the time. Besides, if anyone knew what I was feeling it would be her. She had her own future to think about. There's no way she wouldn't understand when I had to leave.

The moment I laid eyes on her all logic seemed irrelevant. She'd changed out of her scrubs after work and was wearing a pair of shorts and one of those drape-y shirts that girls liked now. It clung to her breasts and flared at her hips, skimming her thighs and making me consider how soft it would be under my hands.

"Hey," she said warmly. Her bare feet were propped on a rung at the island stool. There was something so sweet about how naked they were that had me stopping in the entryway. The words I'd so carefully considered evaporated.

"Hey," was all I could manage.

Before I could say anything else, she got to her feet and said, "I have some news."

I let out a breath. Here was my chance. "So do I, but you first."

She took a sip from the glass of wine in her hand. "I was accepted for the volunteer position."

"That's amazing! I had no doubt you would be."

I closed the distance between us, unable to hear her say anymore. I should be happy for her, but all I could think about was how empty my apartment would be when she was gone.

There was a long silence. I could tell she expected me to fill it, but I still didn't know what to say. "What about you? What's your news?" she asked.

I glanced at my watch, unable to look her in the eye. "Don't worry about it. We'd better get going or we're going to be late for Taco and Tequila Tuesday with your friends. I think we should celebrate your good news first. We can talk about this after."

"Are you sure?" she asked. "You're acting weird."

"I'm sorry. It's just been a long day. I could use some of that tequila."

A COUPLE HOURS and several shots of tequila later, I'd

pushed the email, the future and everything but Charlie out of my mind.

I couldn't get enough of her. Enough of looking at her, talking to her, kissing her. I spent most of the night imagining just what I'd do to her once I got her alone.

Tripp shoved my shoulder. "Someone's whipped," he joked. "Were you even listening to me?"

"Fuck you. You and I both know I'm not the only whipped individual here." I glanced pointedly at Ember, and Tripp sighed and sipped his beer. Taking pity on him, I changed the subject. "What were we talking about?"

"Graduation. How does it feel to finally have freedom on the horizon?"

The immediate answer should have been resoundingly enthusiastic, and would have been a couple months ago, but now, all I could think about was Charlie and leaving her behind. "It's good, man."

Tripp quirked a brow. "Well now I'm just overcome. C'mon man, seriously, what the fuck? I thought you vet school all lined up."

I sipped my beer and wished it were another shot of tequila. "I did, I mean I do."

"Well, spill, dude. Where did you accept?"

I sighed. "I had a couple of places I was considering."

"You don't sound too excited."

"No, I am. They're a great opportunity. All really good schools."

"I'm happy for you, dude."

"Thank you." He lifted his beer to knock it against mine, but for some reason, I no longer felt like celebrating.

I down the beer anyway and went in search of Charlie. I needed to see her, hold her. I had to tell her about school at some point, but I wanted to make this moment last a little longer.

I found her playing Cards Against Humanity with Layla, Ember, and Ember's neighbor and rival Dash. They were falling over each other with laughter, faces bright from the tequila shots they'd been doing and stacks of messy cards in front of them. Charlie caught my eye and motioned for me to come sit next to her on the couch. Just being near her soothed me.

As I watched them play, I tried to remember if it had been the same way when we were just friends. It must have at least been similar, otherwise we wouldn't have been so drawn together for so long. Which made me wonder if we were together because we were such good friends or were we friends because this thing between us was so strong.

An hour later, I propped her up with one arm as we stumbled our way outside to an Uber We'd both had one too many tequila shooters and after a couple rounds of cards had started giggling at every damn thing.

"Did you know your hair is just the cutest thing?" she squealed as I carried her out of the Uber to my front door. Tripp and Dash were following behind with my car. Tripp because it was spring training and he couldn't drink much, Dash because he didn't drink—at all. Ever. When I'd asked, Charlie wouldn't say.

"My hair, huh?" I said and had to fight to keep her hands from wandering all over my body—at least until we got behind closed doors.

"I like having you around," she said when we stumbled inside. "You're like a sexy, snuggly bear."

"Oh, am I?"

Her giggle was muffled as she started kissing her way down my chest. Finally, I gave up trying to let her walk to the door while she was so distracted and simply picked her up again. This both helped and hindered because she was able to focus completely on kissing, licking, and nipping at my skin instead of walking, but I grew more and more distracted the longer she went at it.

"Jesus Christ, Charlie. You're killing me."

"I want you naked, Liam. You're wearing too many clothes." She said the last bit in my ear on a moan.

I was about ready to break the damn door down when it finally opened. I wanted it to last forever. I wanted to spread her out underneath me and take her slowly, torturously, but that's not what happened. We slammed into the apartment, the front door flying back and crashing against the wall.

"There goes your security deposit," Charlie said against my mouth.

"You mean there goes your security deposit."

"I didn't pay a security deposit for this place," she reminded me as I sampled her throat.

"Clearly and oversight on my part. Fine, we'll split any damages."

I felt her laugh vibrate against my tongue. "So chivalrous, Mr. Walsh."

Careful to catch her head with one hand, I guided her back against the wall and kicked the door close with my foot. "That's me, baby."

She snorted. "I'll believe that when I see it."

I carried her to the bedroom, then followed her down onto the bed and for a while, nothing mattered but the sighs and moans I stole from her.

~

"WHAT'S THIS?"

I cracked open an eye to find Charlie standing by the bed. She was holding my phone.

Shit.

I sat up and pressed my fingers to my eyes, hoping the pause before I had to respond would give me time enough to come up with an explanation. "What are you doing?"

"Your phone kept ringing. I got up to get a glass of water and turn it off." Her voice was still hoarse from the shouting at Ember's place and then all the shouting I'd made her do after. "You got accepted to UF?"

I didn't want to lie to her. Couldn't. So I said simply, "Yes."

"I also saw you applied to California. You never told me."

I sat up and pulled the sheet over my lap along the way as I leaned against the headboard. "I applied to schools all over the country. California was just one of them. I can't afford to go there, so I accepted UF."

She'd pulled on one of my shirts. It bagged around her and flirted with her legs. It made her look young and vulnerable. And hurt. Fuck, I didn't want to hurt her. That was the last thing I wanted to do. But I had and it was already killing me.

"Why didn't you tell me?"

"It just happened. I was going to tell you." I lifted a shoulder. "I just couldn't figure out what to say. Besides, you're leaving this summer, too."

"Were you?" Gone was the laughter, the bright eyes. Her lips were pressed into a hard line and the angry furrow between her brows was one I'd never really had directed at me.

"Why wouldn't ?"

"Actually, I turned down the position. You didn't give me a chance to say it earlier, but I was planning to stay." The only other time I'd ever heard her voice sounding so dead was the day she told me her father had died. "For you."

"You shouldn't have done that," I answered honestly. I

never wanted her to give up her plans for me. That wasn't the Charlie I knew.

"Well, I did. Because you made me realize it wasn't the only important thing in my life." She was doing that thing where she tried to be strong, but I heard the reed-thin sound to her voice. "It's ironic, isn't it? The one guy I fall for and actually think won't hurt me is the one who hurts me the worst."

"Don't say that." All my life, I'd been working to prove myself to my father. I'd dealt with the guilt from leaving my family, abandoning Grandma Dorothy. Charlie knew this. And yet the moment I saw her take a step away from me as I sat up to go to her, I would have given up everything I'd earned to have her happy again.

"Why not? It's the truth."

I shifted under the sheet. "Believe me or not, but I was gonna tell you. Last night just wasn't the right time."

Her voice hardened. She was turning to stone right in front of my eyes. Because of me. "How long have you known?"

"Does it matter?" There was no way she'd forgive me now.

"It matters to me."

"Look Charlie, things between us are still new. We're still getting used to...whatever this is. I didn't want to ruin anything."

"Don't you think moving halfway across the country is

going to have an impact on whatever this is?" Normally the snarky tone she'd take when she argued would bring a smile to my face, but this time it made my stomach sink.

"Can we not talk about this now? It's early and we're both tired." And the last thing I wanted to do was have a conversation that could possibly bring about the end of us when we'd barely even begun.

She was silent for a long moment. Long enough that I thought maybe she'd agree to drop it. Then she moved quickly to tug on her jeans and slip into her flats. She was still wearing my shirt. For some reason that stood out in my mind. Like as long as she still had something of mine we'd always be connected.

"What are you doing?" I asked, sitting straight up.

"I think it's best if I leave. I'm gonna go stay at a hotel for the night. While you're at work tomorrow, I'll pack up so I won't be here when you get back."

"Wait a damn minute." I wanted to get up, to stop her, but she was already slinging her purse over her shoulder. By the time I hopped up and drug on a pair of sweats, she was already striding to the front door.

"Don't worry about it, Liam. We'll figure everything out when you get back."

"Dammit, Charlie. What are you doing?" Thunder rolled and I had to raise my voice over it.

"I'm leaving you before you have to make the hard decision to leave me first. I knew this was a stupid thing for me to do and I did it anyway. For you."

Then she spun around and slammed out the door before I could tug on my shoes and follow her. By the time I reached my truck, she was already peeling out into the heavy downpour of the sudden Florida storm. My hands fused to my steering wheel as I followed her out into the rain and onto the highway. All I could picture was her face and how I didn't want it to be the way we ended things.

CHAPTER TWENTY FIVE

CHARLIE

THE RAIN SUITED MY MOOD. I wanted to drown in it, hide in it. But most of all, I wanted to run...and I hated myself for it. I thought of my mom and realized maybe I really was just like her. The second I saw Liam's acceptance letter it was like the floor had been torn right out from under me. I wanted to scream and cry and rage, so I did. In between stop lights and on long stretches of road. I screamed and tears poured from my eyes. It was so early, there was barely any traffic.

There was no one to see me break down. No one to save me now that I'd left the one person who'd always been there.

I was truly alone now.

I took a curve going a little too fast and slightly tapped the brakes. At first I thought it was my car. Maybe the damn thing had finally given up the ghost, but no. My car skidded across the rain-slick streets and began to hydroplane across three lanes of traffic, right in front of the semi in the inside lane next to me.

Even though my head screamed at me not to slam my foot on the brakes, my body reacted without thought. All I could think was I needed to stop before I slammed through the guard rail and into oncoming traffic. Everything happened so fast, but slow at the same time. The time in which I spent spinning across two lanes of traffic on the interstate and then into the grassy median seemed to take an eternity.

I braced for impact, but the muddy grass slowed me down —or maybe it was the death-stomp I had on the brake. Either way, my car came to a sickening halt facing north on the southbound side of the interstate.

Rain pelted against the hood of my car and sweat dampened my brow, my upper lip, and the backs of my knees in hot, uncomfortable pinpricks. At the same time, I trembled, skin coated in goosebumps from the chill. I was alive.

Then shock settled in and my hands began to quake.

I'd spent my whole life being strong. First for my dad after my mom split, then for myself when I was all alone in the world. I didn't want to be strong anymore. I didn't want to do it all on my own. I wanted someone I could trust to lean on, and maybe that's why I took the news about Liam's leaving so hard. I thought he was the one I could trust to always be there.

But now, none of that seemed important.

I was scared and alone and all I wanted was his arms around me to tell me it would be okay.

I fumbled in my purse for my phone to call emergency services to help with my car and report the accident, and to call Liam and apologize for overreacting. God, I wanted to apologize. But my phone was dead and I'd left my charger at his house when I'd raced out. The tears spilled over then and I banged my head against the steering wheel.

I forced myself to breathe normally—in through my nose and out through my mouth—until I calmed down enough to think rationally. Someone would have reported the accident. Someone would see my car stuck on the side of the road and they'd call the state troopers. I'd just need to wait until someone came out to check on me. Then I'd figure out what to do from there.

It didn't take long for the flash of someone's headlights to shine into my front window. Certainly faster than I thought their response time would be, considering the torrential downpour. Their lights were shining into my eyes, so I couldn't see who it was, but it didn't matter. I was grateful.

Unable to keep my head up any longer—crashing from the adrenaline, I guessed—I slumped against the wheel again as I waited for whoever it was to come to me. Normally, I would have gotten out to meet them, but I wasn't sure I could walk, let alone do so in the early morning in the rain.

My door flew open. "Charlie?"

The sound of Ember's voice sent a shock throughout my whole body, giving me enough energy to sit up. "Ember?"

For a second I was legitimately afraid I'd died. My thoughts were like sludge and it didn't occur to me that there'd be any other explanation.

"Jesus. Are you okay?" I started to move to get out, but she stopped me. "Wait until I can check you over really quick. Do you feel any pain anywhere?" Her fingers came away bloody as she inspected the wound on my head I only just realized was there.

I reached my own hand up and found a sizable bump on my temple that was freely bleeding. "It's just a bump. I'm okay." When there were no significant injuries, she helped me to her SUV to finish the exam rather than wait in the freezing rain. She must have gotten the emergency call when I'd gone off the road. I spotted the semi driver talking to a cop in the distance. I'd have to remember to thank him.

She frowned. "You're okay when I say you're okay. Stay still while I examine you." As her fingers poked and prodded, I stayed as still as possible.

"I'm fine. I promise." The sight of blood cleared my thoughts a little.

"What are you doing out here, Charlie?" Ember asked quietly as she bandaged the wound.

There was no point in trying to hide anything from her. She'd had too much experience dragging out the truth from her mischievous siblings for lies to work on her. "Liam and I had a fight."

She sighed and pulled me in for a hug, then shoved me back firmly to glare. "And you thought the smart thing to do would be go for a drive in the middle of a damn hurricane!"

I nearly rolled my eyes, but I didn't think she'd appreciate it. "This is Florida, there's always a hurricane."

"Be serious. You could have been killed. I've had to see a lot as an EMT, but what I never want to see is someone I love at a call." It was her serious tone that sobered me up.

"I'm sorry, Ember. I would never want to put you through that. To be honest, I was just driving. I didn't know where else to go." I hated to admit that, to be so vulnerable with anyone, but Liam seemed to have opened a damn of emotion I'd never realized had even been there.

Ember took my hand with hers. "You always have somewhere to go. With me, or with Layla. We love you, Charlie, so much. That's why we're friends. We don't have Liam's abs or his dimple, but we love you and you're always welcome with us."

I laughed, but it caused my head to ache and I winced. "Don't make me laugh, it hurts."

"We're gonna take a ride to the hospital to get that checked out, then you're coming home with me."

I opened my mouth to whine about going to the hospital, but one stern look from Ember had me shutting it. No wonder the twins shut up whenever she barked an order. She had the mom glare down pat.

～

LAYLA WAS WAITING for me at Ember's apartment by the time we finished up at the hospital. I felt bad for making them cater to me at the crack of dawn, but at the same time, I don't know what I would have done without them. Which only made me dissolve into tears on Ember's loveseat. Quiet tears, that is, because the twins were asleep in the next room.

"Do you need more ibuprofen?" Ember asked as she leaned over to check the ugly ass bandage on my head.

"No, Mom, I'm fine." Then I sighed. "Speaking of, I have something to tell you guys."

I caught them up on the call from my mother and her offer to push through my application as well as the fallout.

"You're kidding!" Layla gasped.

"Unfortunately, no." The medicine helped, but the combination of a hangover, the knock on the head and the on-and-off crying left me wrung out and my head aching.

"You've been busy," Ember said after checking on her siblings, who thankfully hadn't been disturbed by my arrival after their sitter left.

"You could say that."

"Do you want to talk about Liam?" Layla asked gently.

At the mention of him, my heart twisted in my chest. "I'm not sure what there is to talk about."

Ember handed me a cup of hot coffee. She knew me so well. "We assumed after Layla's mom's mixer that something was going on between you two."

"It's okay if you don't want to talk about it," Layla added hastily after taking her own mug.

"It sounds like it happened so fast, because the physical aspect did, but we've been friends for so long it felt natural to move on to something more."

"I always thought there was something between you two," Ember said as she sat next to me on the loveseat.

"You did?" I asked.

"Duh," Layla answered with a laugh. "You both fit together so well. The only reason we never said anything was because you didn't seem ready to settle down. It would have been a disaster if you dated before you were ready."

"You mean like now?" I stared down into my steaming cup.

"No," Ember rushed to say. "Not at all. You never would have rushed into anything with Liam if you weren't serious about it."

Layla nodded. "No way you'd risk it unless you really care about him. You do care about him, don't you?"

"I do. Much more than I ever thought possible."

"So what happened? You both seemed fine at the party." Ember asked.

My whole body hurt remembering our argument, and not just the residual aches and pains from the accident. "I don't know. I didn't mean to blow up about it, really. I just woke up and saw the notification on his phone that he'd been accepted to all these schools. Schools as far away as California, apparently and he'd never said a word about it to me."

Layla frowned. "He didn't tell you where he was going?"

I shook my head and took a sip of coffee and nearly groaned. Ember understood my love for all things caffeine. Since she often took calls at all hours of the night, she knew the horror of settling for gas station slop and made it a point to make the good stuff whenever she could. "I hadn't even thought of it because I was so focused on how good things were going. Maybe that's why he waited. I don't know. Maybe it's a good thing this happened."

"What are you going to do about volunteering?" Layla asked.

My eyes felt like they'd been filled with sand and then set on fire. I needed about a month of sleep. Maybe that would help the ache that had taken up residence in my heart. "I'm not sure. I've never been in this position before. Part of me gave up going for him, which was something I said I'd never do." Before they could pipe up, I added, "And don't you dare tell me never say never."

"I think this is a good thing," Ember declared.

"You do?" Layla and I said at the same time.

"Yes, I do. You've been so closed off for so long, there was bound to be someone who broke you out of your shell. Even better that it was Liam, who we already know is a good guy."

"But he lied to her," Layla said with a scowl.

"He's probably just as confused as she is. Relationships are hard enough without being friends first."

Layla and I both held our tongues. Ember and her boyfriend had been together for years, but things had been rocky since he started university in Miami. Long distance had been rough on them both.

I sighed. "I don't know what to do."

"You don't have to make any decisions now," Layla said, ever the reasonable one. "Take a couple days and figure out your next step. You both owe it to each other to work through the first hiccup. If you decide you don't want to keep being with him, you don't."

"What if I do...and he doesn't?" I almost couldn't get the words out. The coffee had cooled, but I no longer wanted it. The taste was acrid on my tongue.

What if I'd finally fallen for someone and got my heart broken? I'd spent so long running away from being hurt again that I was terrified to stop. Then Liam had kissed me and I'd forgotten to be afraid, if only momentarily.

Ember rubbed my back. "Then we'll be here for you. No matter what happens, you aren't alone, Charlie. Why don't you get some rest? We'll figure everything out in a couple hours."

"I don't know how to thank you guys."

"You don't have to thank us," Layla said as she crossed to me and kissed my brow. "We're your friends. No matter what."

"You can take my room that way the monsters don't bother you," Ember added.

I looked at my two friends and ordered myself not to cry again. "I don't know how to thank you."

"You don't have to thank us," Layla said cheerfully. "We fully expect payback whenever if and when our shit hits the fan."

"I'll remember that," I said as I stumbled my way down the hall to Ember's room.

I collapsed on her bed and wrapped myself in her sheets. As my eyes shuttered closed all I could think about was Liam. Too tired to cry anymore, I hugged a pillow close to my chest and fell asleep imagining it was him I was holding instead.

CHAPTER TWENTY SIX

LIAM

I DROVE AROUND in the rain for hours looking for her. I checked all of her favorite hangouts, her job. I even arrived for her first early-morning class, but she wasn't there and none of her other classmates had seen her.

Walking back to my truck, having no idea where she could be, I was damn sure I couldn't get any lower. My phone beeped with a message.

Tripp: Yeah, I've seen her. Ember mentioned Charlie's staying at her place for a couple days. Why, what's up?

Me: Thx, man. I'll explain later.

The screen went black in my hands as I sat in the cab of my truck with the rain pouring down. I slammed the phone against the steering wheel until I heard something crack and then threw it in the floor well on the passenger side.

"Fuck!" I shouted.

I never wanted to hurt her. I promised myself before this ever started that I wouldn't. The look on her face...I'd rather she'd scream at me...hit me...anything other than the look she gave me before she left. Like I'd betrayed her.

I drove home in a fog, barely noticing the downpour, and only making it there out of pure luck. Her parking space was empty. The house was quiet without her in it and I'd never noticed how much she seemed to fill the space until she was gone.

~

TWO WEEKS.

Two weeks and I hadn't heard from Charlie.

Well, other than to come home one afternoon after classes and realize some of her stuff was gone. I'd texted Tripp and he confirmed Ember and Layla had come by to pick up some of her things. I could barely spend any time in the apartment without being bombarded with memories of her.

I took a page from her book and fled for the first weekend I had free from my new job. I couldn't stand coming home and her not being there with food on the stove and a smile the second I opened the door. My bed was cold without her splayed across it. For a guy who'd spent several years chomping at the bit to leave a house full of women, I found myself aching to have her back.

And it pissed me off.

I tempted highway patrol by speeding the whole way home, but I didn't pass the first trooper. It left me itching for a fight.

And I knew just where I could get one.

Orange dust streamed behind me as I drove a little too fast on the dirt road that led to what was soon to be someone else's land. The thought didn't help me calm down. I ground my teeth together and knotted my hands on the wheel, the leather scrunching in protest under my fists.

I pulled into the front yard and parked next to my dad's truck. He was home. Good.

Metal shrieked as I slammed my door, but instead of my dad greeting me at the door, I found Grandma Dorothy, her round face upturned as she grinned in pleasure.

"Liam!" she said. She hadn't recognized me without prompting in longer than I could recall and it stopped me in my tracks on the top step. "It's so good to see you."

The hinges of the screen door groaned as I pulled it open to wrap my arms around her waist. She only came up to my chest, but when she encircled my waist with her arms, I felt seven-years-old again. Except she couldn't heal all my hurts with Kool-Aid and cartoons anymore.

"Missed you, Gram," I said as I bent down and pressed my lips to her hair.

"Missed you, too," she replied.

"Shouldn't you be at school?" A derisive snort followed the question.

"Don't start," Mom said with a stern look in my father's direction as she pushed past him and tugged me through down the hall. Gram followed close behind, humming. Mom pushed me into a chair at the table. "Something's wrong. Want tea?"

She was already making a glass before I could answer. "Nothing's wrong. I'm fine."

"Son, I've had twenty-two years of deciphering your moods. I can tell when you're upset." She set the glass of iced tea down on the table in front of me. Now you tell me what it is, or I'll beat it out of you."

Grandma Dorothy sat opposite me and Dad skulked in behind, but veered off for his recliner in the attached den. I ignored him, but I could feel his presence like the threat of a malignant tumor or a lurking aneurysm. It was only a matter of time before one of us blew up at the other.

"Charlie and I had an argument." I had to take a couple deep swallows of tea to get around the knot in my throat. "She moved out."

Mom laid a hand on my shoulder. "I'm so sorry. What happened?"

The words burned in my chest. I took another sip of tea. "I didn't tell her something important and it hurt her."

Grandma Dorothy began waving one hand and the other

tapped monotonously against the table. I could almost feel Dad straining to hear from the other room.

"What was it?" Mom asked.

I sighed and the bunched muscles in my shoulder wound a little tighter. "About my plans for school next year. I applied to some schools out of state. We—" my throat closed around the words. I cleared it with another swallow of tea. "We'd gotten...closer since she moved in. I care about her—I love her. And I let her down."

Dad snorted so loud, we could hear it from the kitchen.

"Ignore him," Mom ordered. Grandma Dorothy's humming increased in volume. "You haven't heard from her?"

"No, and I don't blame her. I should have talked to her about it, but things were going so good I didn't want to ruin them. Then I got denied for the scholarship," I said a little more loudly, "and I had to figure a lot of things out at once. She saw the information on my phone and it just blew up from there."

Silence from the den. *Good.*

Grandma Dorothy continued to hum.

"Poor girl," Mom said as she sat next to me at the table. "She's been through so much. She's probably just scared. She's lost everything. I'm sure she was just afraid of losing you, too."

I hung my head. "I know. I know that more than anyone. I was a fucking idiot."

"Language," Mom admonished. "Just give her time. If you

love her, you'll know what to do when the time is right. When you love someone you learn to put up with all of their bull-headed actions!" she shouted toward Dad.

"Thanks, Mom." I leaned over and kissed her cheek. "How are things around here?" I nodded in grandma's direction.

"They'd be better if she could stay home," Dad thundered as he stalked to the fridge for a beer.

Mom gave me a pointed look that said to ignore him, but my blood heated at his words and my brain was screaming at me to engage. This was the fight I'd been spoiling for.

"A nursing home would be more secure. She needs more care then you'll be able to provide," I said.

The beer can hissed as he popped the tab. "We could handle her just fine here if we had you to help out in the fields instead of wasting time at that school."

"Only an idiot would think getting an education was a waste of time," I said through clenched teeth.

Grandma shoved up from the table and began pacing.

"Watch your mouth," Dad barked. "We're a family. You support your family."

I got to my feet. "Support, huh? Where was your support when the first child in the family decided to go to college to get a degree? Where was your support when I needed that scholarship? That goes both ways, *Dad*, in case you didn't know."

He took a step closer and my mom got to her feet, her

chair scraping against the dingy linoleum. "Willy, don't," she warned.

We both ignored her. "You think you know everything. That you can do everything without your family's help. You know nothing, son. You left for school and suddenly you had no responsibilities here. Your sisters, your mother, your grandmother. They didn't factor in to your big plans. Now everything I've worked for the past forty years is gone."

I flinched. "You want to blame me for it all going to shit, but I'm not the problem, Dad. The farm was struggling long before I decided I didn't want to go down with it. You just don't want to admit it and now you're punishing me for your failures."

"You think you can just wash your hands of your responsibilities and think it's done. I thought better of you, but I guess I was wrong. I never thought I'd see the day when I was ashamed of my son."

That hurt more than I wanted to admit. "I don't need your approval. I guess I should have known better than to ask you to help me in any way. Consider me dead to you, Dad, since you're so ashamed. You won't ever have to worry about my choices again."

"Willy! Liam! Stop this nonsense," Mom ordered.

I took a step back toward the hall. It had been me who'd instigated the confrontation, hoping it would make the hole in my chest go away, but if anything, it had made it bigger.

When I looked back to Dad, prepared for another verbal

assault, he was no longer glaring at me. Instead, his head was on a swivel and he'd lost all color in his face.

"Mom?" His voice broke. "Mom?" He said a little louder.

The humming and pacing had stopped.

And the back door was open.

Gram was gone.

CHAPTER TWENTY SEVEN

CHARLIE

THINGS THAT HAD ONCE GIVEN me pleasure no longer did.

Coffee, even, had failed me.

I stared down at my mug listlessly and then poured it back in the sink. My stomach couldn't handle anything lately, anyway. Apparently a symptom of heartache was constant nausea. Pregnancy had occurred to me, briefly, but my period was regular as always. A baby was the last thing either of us needed. The thought of a mini Liam, however, only made me cry harder in my pillow that night. Maybe it was hormones.

"You seem sad. Problems with your young man again?" Mr. Williams asked as I contemplated my next move.

Sighing, I chose a piece at random and moved it blindly. I almost laughed because that's exactly how I've been feeling since I walked out of Liam's apartment. Everyone around me seemed to have a plan and I was operating blind, unaware of the rules. In a short time, Liam had managed to redefine all the rules of the game I thought I'd played like a champ.

"You could say that," I said.

He smiled knowingly. "Life's too short. I've told you a thousand times."

Didn't I know it. "You say that, but you've been sweet on Mrs. Agnes for months now and haven't made a move."

"I'm laying the groundwork," he said and captured one of my rooks.

"Sure you are," I replied and smiled for the first time in what felt like weeks as I moved a castle. "Check."

"Think about this question, and then I'll leave it alone. In ten years, when you look back on this moment, will you regret the choices you're making? You'll know the answer then. There are some things we just *know* that no amount of reasoning will explain." Then, he captured my queen and said, "Checkmate."

APRIL WAS WAITING for me a couple hours later when I got off work.

At first, I considered ignoring her completely, but then I decided I was through running. If a tendency to be conflict avoidant was learned, I was going to be the one who unlearned it.

She was dressed in a skirt with matching jacket that was as pristine and polished as fine art. Nothing like the stay-at-home-mom I remembered, now that I studied her long enough to draw comparisons.

"April," I said in a flat, careful voice. "What are you doing here?"

She bit her lip and the action reminded me so much of myself it took my breath away. "I wanted to apologize. I shouldn't—I shouldn't have pushed you the way I did."

I crossed my arms over my chest. "No," I said bluntly, "you shouldn't have."

"I'm sorry, I jumped in too fast. I have no right to butt into your life."

Spotting coworkers down the hall, I nodded to the exit. "Can we do this outside?" I led her to the parking lot where we'd have more privacy. Heat shimmered up from the asphalt, but there was a cool breeze that calmed my frazzled nerves. "No, you don't have a right to butt into my life. Don't get me wrong, I appreciated your help, but you have no idea who I am or who Liam is for that matter."

April nodded. "I agree. I only saw so much of myself in you and I didn't want you to make the same mistakes I did when I was your age. I gave up so much for your father and I lost so much of *me* in the process."

The teeth of my keys bit into my palm. "I'm sure you had your reasons, but if we're going to have any sort of relationship, you need to respect my choices."

"Of course," she said immediately. "It won't happen again."

The coil of nerves in my stomach loosened. "Good. Thank you."

"Would you—I mean, I'm picking up my daughter in a few minutes from school. Would you like to meet her?"

At a loss for words, I could only gape.

"Only if you want to," she hurried to add. "No pressure, I promise."

This was the moment. I could either walk away and continue to let these past wounds fester—on both our parts—or I could stop running.

Thinking about Mr. Williams and Liam, there was no choice. No thinking. No panic.

For the first time in my life, I felt free, a weight lifted off my shoulders.

"I'd love to."

The smile she gave me brought out a mirror grin from me.

I WAS STILL LAUGHING as I waved goodbye to April and my half-sister Madison. I had a sister! Grandparents! A mom. I'd lost so much that I didn't quite know what to do with myself as I drove home feeling like I was full up to the brim with happiness.

Except, there was no one for me to share it with.

Well, there was, but I wasn't sure if he'd ever want to speak to me again.

All I wanted to do was take the route that would lead me back to his—our—apartment and tell him all the things I'd learned today.

Ember and Layla had been begging me to talk to him and work things out, but I hadn't mustered up the nerve. I wasn't sure if I forgave him until I'd been able to forgive my mother. I felt lighter than I had in years. I didn't think I could have gotten this far if it weren't for him.

Acting on instinct, I flipped on my blinker and ignored the resulting angry drivers honking at me as I switched lanes. *Screw it.* I was going to go see him. My heart raced as I navigated my way through the afternoon traffic to Lake Ella and then to Liam's duplex.

I pulled up the drive and slumped in my seat when I noted the absence of his truck. He wasn't home. He was probably working. Feeling a little deflated, I parked and tried to figure out my next move.

My phone rang and figuring it was probably Ember checking in again, I answered it without looking at the caller I.D. "Yes, I'm fine, Em. I'll be back in a little while."

"Charlie? It's Mrs. Walsh."

"Mrs. Walsh. Is Liam okay?" I'd gotten a call like this before. My heart was in my throat along with my breakfast.

"Liam's fine. It's Grandma Dorothy." I stopped breathing, wanted to tell her to stop talking, but she continued. "Oh, honey, I hate to have to tell you this over the phone, but she passed away."

CHAPTER TWENTY EIGHT

LIAM

I'D NEVER FORGET the smell of the hospital.

I thought Charlie was crazy when she talked about how it smelled like death and antiseptic. But I got it now. The scent was burned into my nose and now every time I thought of Gram, all I'd remember was the smell of the room where they took me to I.D. her body. My mother had been hysterical, and dad hadn't argued when I told him to stay with her and my sisters at home. A testament to his shock, because there hasn't been a day in the past couple years when Dad *didn't* argue with me.

"Mr. Walsh?"

"Yeah?" I lifted my head and found a nurse or assistant or doctor. My eyes were too bloodshot and blurry to even bother trying to read their nametag.

"Is there anyone I can call for you?"

I gave half a thought to calling Charlie, but decided

against it. I wouldn't know what to say to her and God, the thought of telling her about Gram had my throat closing in on itself.

"No, thanks." I knew I needed to get back home, so I got to my feet and shoved my hands into my jeans. The nurse nodded and sent me a sad smile before padding back to the nurse's station.

My legs worked well enough to carry me back to my truck, which was parked haphazardly outside the guest entrance to the hospital. I guess a part of me had thought if I got here quick enough maybe I could have saved her. Which didn't make any sense now, but it had then. I'd driven like a maniac with my hazards on, but I was too late.

Looking back so many decisions I'd made were stupid. Unimportant. Reckless.

I drove to my parents on auto-pilot. I'd been up nearly forty-eight hours, but I knew there'd be no sleep for me tonight. There was so much we still needed to do.

My exhaustion and mental and emotional numbness had me staring dumbly at the car next to my parents' vehicles in the driveway. I knew I recognized it, but it took a few minutes for realization to dawn. It was Charlie's car.

Despite how much I wanted her there with me, I took my time getting out of the truck and heading to the front door. I almost didn't want to face what was on the other side. I didn't think I could handle losing both her and Gram at the same time. There's strength and then there's a breaking point and if losing Gram had taught me anything it was my limits. To be humble. That I didn't control everything. Or know everything for that matter.

The soaps Gram used to play non-stop in the front room weren't on, which made the house all too quiet as I made my way back to the kitchen. It hurt to be here. My chest ached with it and my throat was as dry as our fields after a drought.

Sunlight spilled in from the window above the kitchen sink and when I entered the kitchen, it seemed to surround Charlie like a halo. I noticed my parents out of the corner of my eye, but all I could see was Charlie.

She'd been crying and that undid all my self-control. I crossed the room to her, determined to beg her forgiveness, when she opened her arms and took me into them. I breathed her in, the sweet green apple scent of her washing away the memories of the hospital.

"Liam," she said, her voice full of emotion. "I'm so sorry."

I couldn't even speak, I just nodded even though I'd pressed my face to the curve of her neck. I had to bend my knees since she was so short, but I didn't care. I'd been damn sure I'd never see her again, so a little discomfort was worth having her in my arms. Footsteps scraped against the floor as my parents left, but I didn't let her go to check.

"Let's go to your room," she said as she rubbed my back. I nearly groaned at how good it felt to have her hands on me again. When I wouldn't let her go, she laughed a little. "Okay, big guy," and then maneuvered us out of the kitchen and down the hall with me still clinging to her like a stubborn child.

Charlie frog-marched us down the hall to the spare room that used to be mine when I was younger. My parents had since converted it to a guest room. Clothes and a tangle of cords spewed from the open mouth of the backpack I'd tossed haphazardly on the bed. I was acting like a little bitch, but I could only watch as she carefully cleared off the clutter and turned down the sheets.

"What are you doing here?" My voice sounded like I deep throated a chainsaw. *Christ.*

She nibbled on her lip. "I'm sorry, I should have asked you if it was okay before I came, your mom was just so upset I drove straight over here."

"You don't have to apologize, Charlie. She was yours, too." There was so goddamn much I wanted to say, but I could barely keep my eyes open. My brain had registered Charlie and the bed and all I wanted to do was curl up on it with her, but I didn't dare ask.

"Well, that's a conversation we'll have to have when you aren't falling asleep on your feet," she said. I thought she might have been smiling, but my vision had blurred until she was nothing but a teal-green blur in her work scrubs. "Let's get you into bed."

I would have cracked a joke if my brain had the ability to form a coherent sentence. All I could manage was falling face-first into the pillows. "Stay with me," I tried to say, but into the pillows, it came out more, "Starlf bith be."

"What?" she asked.

There was enough energy left in me to life my head. "Stay with me," I repeated. "Please." I'd beg if she wanted me to.

Charlie hesitated in the doorway. "Are you sure?"

I'd never been more certain about anything. "Please."

There was a long pause while she licked her lips and studied me on the bed. For a few thudding heartbeats, I thought she was going to turn me down. Then, she toed off her shoes and stripped off her socks, then walked across the room to climb over me and settle down under the covers. I switched off the light and thanks to the blackout curtains, the room was plunged into immediate darkness.

"I'm sorry," she said again.

"Me, too," I replied, then decided screw it. I wasn't wasting anymore time. "Can I hold you?"

She sniffled. "Please."

I rolled to my side and wrapped my arms around her. She buried her face into my chest and her body began to shake. Time seemed to slow to a stop as losing Gram hit me all at once. I hadn't allowed myself a second to feel it. From the moment we realized she was gone, to getting the call from the police to inform us of her death, to identifying her body, I'd been stoic. Mom had broken down from the stress of me and Dad fighting. Dad had been overrun by guilt. My sisters, when they'd learned about her going missing, had been inconsolable. I'd been the only one to hold them all together.

"This wasn't your fault," she said against my shirt. "It wasn't."

"She left because me and dad were fighting. We'd flustered her. She left and then forgot how to get home. She was wandering around the streets, lost and alone for hours. She died alone. If someone hadn't seen her, we may have never found her. If I hadn't pushed him so hard, she'd still be alive."

She was silent for a while, then she said, "By that reasoning, if I hadn't taken up so much of Dad's time when I was younger, he would have gone to the doctor sooner, caught the cancer sooner. Maybe he'd still be alive."

I shook my head. "It's not the same thing, Charlie."

"It is," she insisted. "Gram was sick. Very sick. I've talked to your mother about it. She didn't have much longer, even with constant care. It was more a matter of making her as comfortable as possible. It was an accident, Liam."

When I didn't respond, she pulled back and as my eyes adjusted to the dark, I met hers as she studied me. "Do you think she'd blame you? Do you think she'd want her only grandson to shoulder that amount of guilt?"

My immediate answer wasn't one I was willing to consider. "Get some sleep, Charlie," I said instead.

Her free arm came around me as her body settled against mine. For the first time in nearly three weeks, I was able to fall into a deep and dreamless sleep.

"WHY DON'T you git and let that young lady have a moment's peace?" My great-aunt Ida told me as she shoved me away from the refreshment buffet set up in our kitchen after Grandma Dorothy's funeral.

Charlie hadn't leave my side over the past three days. Through funeral arrangements, receiving out of town guests, and the service itself. When I turned, she was there. After the first night of sharing a bed together, I'd moved to the couch and let her have the bed. She didn't bring up resuming our relationship, and I didn't ask. I was simply grateful she hadn't left.

"He's alright," Charlie told her. "Besides, he gets lonely when I leave him alone."

Aunt Ida eyed me over the tuna casserole. "Well, alright, but you let me know if he starts bothering you."

"Yes, ma'am," I will.

"How is it my family likes you better than me?" I asked as I made up my own plate. I wasn't exactly hungry, but my mom was watching me like a hawk and I knew if I didn't eat she'd beeline over to me in a heartbeat.

"I'm much prettier," Charlie answered and popped a grape into her mouth from the fruit platter.

"And so humble," I teased with a grin that felt like it needed to be oiled.

Charlie's eyes softened, and I realized it was the first time

I'd smiled since Grandma Dorothy died. My smile instantly fell, and I took a step toward her, plate of food forgotten on the table. "Charlie, I—"

"Liam, can I talk to you for a minute?" my father interrupted. He stopped short when he realized how close Charlie and I were standing. "It can wait until you're done here."

"No," Charlie said as she pushed me in his direction. "We can talk about this later."

When I opened my mouth to protest, Charlie glared at me. "Fine," I said and followed Dad through the throngs of relatives to the deserted front porch. Good. At least there'd be no witnesses when we had another epic blowout and it devolved to one of us throwing punches. It wouldn't be the first time in the south when fists were raised at a funeral.

I crossed my arms over my chest and leaned against the porch railing. "What did you want to talk about?"

He crumpled onto the porch swing, the metal chains groaning in protest, and buried his head in his hands. "I'm sorry, son. For everything I've said. For what I've done. Mom tried to tell me I was being too hard on you—when she was aware of what was going on. She tried to tell me I was pushing you away, but I didn't listen." He looked up then with a broken smile. "Guess that runs in the family."

I couldn't remember the last time my dad had apologized —to anyone, let alone to me, who'd seemed to disappoint him at every turn. The anger that had seemed to burn a hole in my gut whenever I was I the same room with him had turned to stone. "I'm sorry, too. I got it in my head that I was going to do things my way and I never stopped to consider helping any of you. I thought if I went to school and got my degree I'd be able to make enough money for everyone. Figure we were both equally wrong."

"For what it's worth, I am proud of you, for all you've done. I never could have stuck it out in college and I'm damn proud you're my son."

I looked to my feet, my face heating. "Thanks," I managed to choke out. "That means a lot to me."

"Gram was proud of you, too," he said as he got to his feet and pulled me in for a one-armed hug. "Now let's go find your mom and let her know we made up so she doesn't divorce me. That woman is like your Charlie. I knew I found a good one and didn't give her a second to come to her senses before I chained her down. You'd be wise to do the same."

CHAPTER TWENTY NINE

CHARLIE

"I CAN'T BELIEVE you're leaving me. Who is going to spend Taco and Tequila Tuesdays with us now?" Ember threw herself down onto the couch next to me. Layla nodded enthusiastically from her place on the floor where she was sorting through the mountain of things I'd managed to accumulate at her place. I'd only been living at her place a few weeks, but somehow my things had wound up all over her apartment.

I gave them both quelling looks, which they ignored. "I do have a car, you know. I can come see either of you any time. That includes on Taco and Tequila Tuesdays."

Layla sighed heavily as she folded shirts. "It won't be the same with you gone. We won't be able to come over to see you any time we want. You might as well be on the other side of the city!"

I'd given some thought to staying in the building. Now

that the semester was ending, there were a lot of openings. Students moving out, graduating. I could have my pick if I wanted. But I couldn't imagine putting up with the landlord again. Besides, my new apartment was father from campus, but closer to the hospital where I hoped to apply when I graduated. Call it wishful thinking, but I hoped it would impart good vibes for when I did.

"Who is gonna help me plan to defeat Dash? The internship application is due to the committee by the end of the summer, and I just know he's planning on applying just to spite me. I won't make it through the next three months if you're not here. I may kill him this time. For real."

My heart squeezed at the thought of missing their fighting, and inevitable making up. Layla may not realize it, but Dash was definitely going to apply for the internship—just not for the reasons she thought he was. It almost made me a little misty to think of the wild ride that was in store for my friend. I considered warning her ahead of time but managed to bite my tongue. She'd probably kill me if I ever suggested he only teased her because he wanted to get in her pants.

"Uh, hello!" Ember said, waving a hand around. "I still live here. I can help."

Layla sighed again. "I guess."

Ember threw a pillow at Layla's head. "Jerk."

Liam had been secretive about his plans since the funeral, where we didn't get much chance to talk. I wasn't about to press him for details, not while his family was still grieving.

We still chatted and texted constantly, but it wasn't the same. I missed my best friend. I tried to weasel information out of him on the pretense that I'd be willing to adjust my plans for him, but he vehemently rejected that idea. I had to admit, I loved that he wanted me to follow my dreams. Not that I'd ever tell him that.

I'd even grilled his parents for clues, but they were sworn to secrecy. His mother was so overjoyed with the idea that we might get back together that she'd given me one of her rose bushes for my new apartment. "It's tradition," she'd insisted. It was already turning brown, but I didn't have the heart to tell her I was even more hell on plants than she was.

It was late when I finally convinced Layla and Ember I could handle the last load and promised to invite them to my new place as soon as everything was unpacked. I loaded up the rest of the boxes in Liam's truck. I'd let him borrow my car in return as long as I promised him no less than three hundred times that I wouldn't let anything happen to his baby. I drove across town to his duplex where some of my stuff was still stored.

I had to admit as I walked around double-checking drawers and cabinets the emptiness left me feeling a little tender. So much so that when Liam walked through a short while later, I didn't look up from the cabinet I had my head stuck in.

"How'd it go?" I asked from inside, my voice echoing.

"What the hell are you doing?"

"Checking to make sure we didn't leave anything."

"Like a ten-year-old can of tuna?" he asked. I could hear the smile in his voice mocking me, but even that made me want to cry so I kept my head in the cabinet. He'd packed all his things the week before. I hadn't realized how much it would affect me until I walked in the living room and found all his furniture gone. It was just another reminder that he could be leaving soon.

For a long time.

Without me.

I had to be strong about it. Liam deserved every chance at a happy future and a good career. As much as I loved him, I loved him enough to set him free if that's what he wanted.

"You never know," I said with forced cheerfulness.

"Can you come out of there for a minute? I have some news."

I froze, half in, half out of the cabinet, my ass probably making a delightful display. I gave a passing thought to staying there and never coming out, but my knees started to ache from kneeling on the tile floor. Standing, I noticed the counter had crumbs on it from God-knows-when and decided to give it a good scrub while I was there.

"Charlie, you and I both know you're not this domestic. Stop procrastinating and get your ass over here before I come over there."

I turned, tossing my hair over one shoulder. "Or what, you'll carry me?"

He leveled me with a look. "If I need to."

There was a moment's pause where I considered defying him, but the edgy look in his eye told me not to push it. Besides, it would be better to go ahead and rip the Band-Aid off so I could deal with the fact that the person I loved most in this world would be halfway across the country for the fore-seeable future. Even though I didn't like it, I knew he was right. Whatever he chose, I'd figure out how to deal with it. We'd been just friends before, we could do it again.

"Fine," I said and flounced away, only to realize, too late, that the only piece of furniture we had left in the apartment was his bed. Unwilling to admit defeat, I stomped to his room and plopped down on the bed. If we were going to have this conversation, I'd rather be annoyed than vulnerable. I would be just as unruffled as he was. We were adults with an adult friendship. I could do this.

Except the second I turned to face him and took a steadying breath, my eyes filled with tears. I groaned at my own childishness. This was silly. Even if he did have to move away it wouldn't be forever.

"Aw, sweetheart, don't cry." He pulled me into a hug and pushed my hair away from my face. "This isn't a bad thing."

I sniffled. "I'm not crying. Ignore me."

He wiped away a tear and then settled in to tell me about the new place he was moving to in August. I listened to his voice rumble through his chest and tried to commit it to memory while still paying attention to the actual words. His words tumbled over themselves as he spoke. It sounded like a dream come true. A great city with the best university. Tourist attractions. Nearby beaches. It was everything he'd been hoping for and more because he'd get to do what he loved, finally, with his father's support. I was happy for him, really, I was, but all I wanted to do was cry.

"The best part about it is I won't have to go far away."

"That's good, I'm hap—" I looked up at him, blinking owlishly. "Wait, what?"

His smile was blinding and a little smug. "I decided to enroll at UF instead of taking out loans for California. They offered me a scholarship I couldn't refuse. I know it's not close, but it beats being a continent away."

"You'll be staying in Florida? What? Why?" Maybe I was dreaming.

"You're not dreaming." I must have spoken aloud again. He cupped my cheek with a hand and I closed my eyes, leaning into his touch. Needing it to keep from spinning out of control. "I love it here. I want to be near my family. Near you. It'll allow me to have the best of both worlds."

"But what about the program in California. You were so looking forward to it, I know you were. If this is because of me, then I forbid you from doing it."

He smiled. "You should know by now I do what I want the way I want it. Dad says it's a family trait. I'm sorry, you're stuck with me."

I didn't know whether I should screech for joy or

convince him what a bad idea it was. "Are you sure about this?"

He lifted me to my feet with two hands at my waist, then tipped my chin up to stare deeply into my eyes. "Completely. Tell me I didn't screw things up. Tell me we can work this out over the next couple years. I want to be with you, Charlie. I'll do whatever it takes."

I kissed him, unable to hold back any longer. "You've already got me."

Thank you so much for getting to know Charlie and Liam! I've been aching to tell their story for a long time now and I'm so excited to have the opportunity to share it with you.

I sincerely hope you enjoyed reading this book as much as I enjoyed writing it. If you did, I would greatly appreciate a short review on Amazon or your retailer. Reviews are crucial for any author, and even just a line or two can make a huge difference.

Also in the Series:

Frenemies (Layla & Dash)
Friends with Benefits (Ember & Tripp)

FRENEMIES

Dashiel Hampton is her enemy.

Layla Tate reminds herself of that fact every morning she goes to class and sees his smug face smirking up at her. From grade school to grad school there hasn't been a moment they weren't pitted against each other and she refuses to back down. She hates him from his rock hard abs to his panty-dropping smile.

Revenge will be oh-so-sweet when she's chosen for the new internship that could make or break her career. Until Dash decides he's not giving up without a fight.

Layla Tate is going down.

There is nothing that makes Dash Hampton as happy as the look on Layla's face when she realizes he's won. He lives to drive her crazy because if he can't have her beneath him, then he'll have her any other way he can.

He'll get her to notice him, even if it means stealing the internship from right beneath her nose. Dash won't give up–on the internship...or her.

As they vie to see who will come out on top, they'll have to keep their friends close and their frenemies closer.

ACKNOWLEDGMENTS

To my friend Alana Albertson thank you for the endless nights you've spent encouraging me to not give up, even when that's the only thing I want to do.

To my friend Melissa Fisher thank you for your endless patience for each installment of this book and your keen eye.

To my friend and the best mother in the world, Diane Collins, for giving birth to the best daughter.

To my friend and daughter, Afton Blanchard, thank you for your endless imagination and enthusiasm. You make each day a joy.

To my friend J.C. for reminding me that we don't quit.

To my friends from Nicole's Knockouts who have stood by me every step of the way, thank you for your support and patience. I know I say it all the time, but you are the reason why I put fingers to keys and make these books a reality. You always seem to know just when I want to throw in the towel and are there with an encouraging word and a listening ear. Sometimes I think I'm alone in this journey and then I look up and all of you are there to remind me I'm not.

Authors would be screaming into the black abyss if it wasn't for the hard-working bloggers who promote our work just as passionately as if it were their own. A special thanks to: The Wonderings of One Person, SJ's Book Blog, EscapeN-Books, Books Over Boys, Crystal's Crazy Book Ramblings, Kiki Reader Loves Books, A Cup and a Book, Black Feather Blogger, I HAVE A BOOK OBSESSION, Exposure Book Blog, BookSnuggle, Desire for Lit, Book Haven, Ree Cee's books, and so many more. If I missed you, please don't hesitate to email. I can always update and I want to include everyone! :P

ABOUT THE AUTHOR

Nicole Blanchard is the *New York Times* and *USA Today* bestselling author of gritty romantic suspense and heartwarming new adult romance. She and her family reside in the south along with their two spunky Boston Terriers and one chatty cat. Keep up-to-date on her new releases by subscribing to her newsletter.

facebook.com/authornicoleblanchard

twitter.com/blanchardbooks

instagram.com/authornicoleblanchard

amazon.com/Nicole-Blanchard

bookbub.com/authors/nicole-blanchard

goodreads.com/Nicole_Blanchard

pinterest.com/blanchardbooks

ALSO BY NICOLE BLANCHARD

First to Fight Series

Anchor

Warrior

Survivor

Savior

Honor

Box Set: Books 1-5

Dark Romance

Toxic

Friend Zone Series

Friend Zone

Frenemies

Friends with Benefits

Standalone Novellas

Bear with Me

Darkest Desires

Mechanical Hearts

CPSIA information can be obtained
at www.ICGtesting.com
Printed in the USA
BVOW09s0920060418

512636BV00002B/5/P